# GUNS OF DODGE CITY

Someone had betrayed an Army battalion of innocent men—and they now lay dead, massacred, with useless guns in their hands.

Captain Bob Pryor, sometimes known as the Rio Kid, followed the bloody trail to Dodge City, where the all-powerful gun lords were plotting an even greater evil.

The Rio Kid was heading for a cattle town shootout—with the deck stacked against him.

**Tom Curry** was born in Hartford, Connecticut and graduated from college with a degree in chemical engineering. Leo Margulies, editorial director for N. L. Pines's Standard Magazines, encouraged Tom to write Western stories. In 1936, Margulies launched a new magazine titled *Texas Rangers*. Leslie Scott wrote the first several of these 45,000-word novelettes about Texas Ranger Jim Hatfield, known as the Lone Wolf, published under the house name Jackson Cole. Tom Curry's first Jim Hatfield story was "Death Rides the Rio" in *Texas Rangers* (3/37) and over the succeeding years he contributed over fifty Hatfield tales to this magazine alone. Curry also wrote three of the series novelettes for *Masked Rider Western* and some for *Range Riders Western*. It was in 1938 that Margulies asked Curry to devise a new Western hero for a pulp magazine and Tom came up with Bob Pryor. *The Rio Kid Western* published its first issue in October 1939. Subsequently Curry expanded several of his Rio Kid stories to form novels, published by Arcadia House, with the hero's name changed from Bob Pryor to Captain Mesquite. Possibly Curry's best Western fiction came during the decade of the 1940s, especially in the Jim Hatfield stories and in his Rio Kid novelettes. After Margulies was released from Standard Magazines, Curry quit writing and began a new career in 1951 with Door-Oliver, Inc., that lasted for fourteen years, working in their research and testing laboratory in Westport as accountant, purchasing agent, and customer service representative, making use at last of his chemical engineering degree. When Curry retired from Door-Oliver, he resumed writing Westerns sporadically for Tower Books and Pyramid Books and, later still, for Leisure Books. In October 1969, Margulies informed Curry that he was to be publishing a new digest-sized publication to be titled *Zane Grey Western Magazine* and he wanted Tom to write some new stories to appear in its pages featuring a number of Zane Grey's best known characters. These stories would be published under the house name Romer Zane Grey. Curry put a lot of talent and energy into so many of his Western novelettes, particularly the Rio Kid adventures, and his stories can still intrigue and entertain.

# GUNS OF DODGE CITY

Tom Curry

GUNSMOKE

This hardback edition 2008
by BBC Audiobooks Ltd
by arrangement with
Golden West Literary Agency

ISBN 978 1 405 68250 3

British Library Cataloguing in Publication Data available.

Printed and bound in Great Britain by
CPI Antony Rowe, Chippenham, Wiltshire

# CHAPTER I

## *Death on the Plains*

☐ The carbines of the troopers crackled raggedly, weakly. In the circle of death, on the little mound, half of the company lay quiet forever.

Blue uniforms, with the yellow stripe showing their branch of the service, were dusty from the grit blown by the wind. For it blew over these vast, rolling expanses of the plains without check, rustling the coarse, thick buffalo grass, and now echoing the explosions of many guns.

It was a desperate moment, and there seemed no way out of the sudden trap which had sprung when hundreds on hundreds of painted warriors had appeared from a hidden ravine, a typical cut in the earth on Great Plains.

These were the plains of the Sioux, their hereditary hunting-grounds on which the buffalo and antelope roamed, the meat, housing, medical, clothing and fuel supply of the Plains Indian. To hold that land against the ever-encroaching white man the Sioux were savagely fighting with sheer determination and all the cunning of their race.

The Civil War, with brother fighting against brother, had raged to a decisive end. But the Indian Wars went

5

on without cessation, as they were to continue through decades.

Since 1868, eight years before, when the Black Hills had been taken back by the Government of the United States, the Sioux had been at it with their allies, the Cheyennes and others, fighting stubbornly against spreading settlers, fighting against the railroad which had split their range in half. Again and again the Indians surprised small bands of soldiers or civilians, or attacked an isolated post or home, leaving death and destruction in their wake.

And yet the white man came on. Where one was killed, three sprang up to take his place.

The captain of this troop now on the little mound was still alive, but he had a bullet from a breech-loading, first-class rifle through his shoulder. A Sioux had made the shot. For the Indians were able to get better weapons than the troopers fighting for the government.

"Rio Kid!" the commander called.

His lips were firmly set, but he spoke coolly, bravely. He was a true soldier of his country. His pistol was still in one hand now, though his other arm was limp and blood-soaked.

A young man with keen blue eyes took his carbine from his shoulder and slid over to where the officer lay. But to reach him, the Rio Kid had to crawl around or over half a dozen dead cavalry troopers.

"What do you think, Pryor?" the captain said in a low, pain-filled voice.

Bob Pryor, known from the Mexican border to the Canadian line as the Rio Kid, shrugged non-committally. The present situation was one not foreign to this man, young, although a veteran of many Civil War battles and fights on the Frontier. Nor was it unusual for any officer knowing his bravery that was accented by a deep, inborn recklessness, to look to him for advice.

"The wind's away from the Fort, Captain," Pryor remarked, as though reading the commanding officer's so far unspoken question.

"Yes, yes. It won't carry the sounds. Is there any chance of a man getting through those devils?"

6

The Rio Kid's narrowed blue eyes searched the enemy lines, lingering on the mounted and painted warriors circling about the beleaguered troop. For this moment there was a lull in the fighting. The Indians had drawn off after sweeping in, whooping and shooting, but had fallen back as the accurate fire of those troopers who still could use guns had torn their ranks.

"I might get through, Captain, if my hoss don't get hit in the first five hundred yards," the Rio Kid replied, as coolly as the officer had spoken.

The captain shook his head, but hope was in his eyes.

"I can't order you to try," he said huskily. "You're a civilian scout."

"I'm already on my way, Captain."

The Rio Kid stood up, his lips firmly set. It might be one of Bob Pryor's jobs, acting as a scout for the Army, but never would he refuse to face danger, in any capacity.

*Click—click!* The sudden sound was ominous in its futility.

Captain Drew hardly glanced around, but his mouth was bitter as he cursed under his breath.

"Another dud!" he groaned.

He swung and called:

"Sergeant McGorty! Break out another case of ammunition."

"Yes, sir."

The Rio Kid picked up the bullet which the swearing soldier flung away. It was a dud all right, a cartridge which had failed to explode. There had been so many in the cases this troop carried that the Indians had grown bold and had swept in close, doing terrific damage.

"If it weren't for that," Pryor thought grimly, "they'd have kept off and run when we opened fire."

For he knew the Sioux—knew their fighting tactics. Seldom would they stand against seasoned troops, but with carbine after carbine missing fire, they cannily guessed what had happened, and knew they were comparatively safe.

Nor had Captain Drew dared risk a running retreat. With useless ammunition, that would have been suicide.

There had been no other course than to stand and fight.

Robert Pryor, the Rio Kid, to whom the wounded officer had now turned as the man on whom he could pin his last hope, had been a cavalry officer under Sheridan and Custer in the Civil War, though now he was no longer in the Army. He was, however, working with it as a civilian scout.

He had been Custer's aide, and was a genius at scouting. He had learned this early in life, as a boy in his home on the Rio Grande, and that knowledge had been invaluable during the Civil War. He had brought it into use on the Frontier after the War had ended, continuing the reputation he had earned as a man who was brave, dependable, fighting always on the side of right. And about him was an impressive air, that of a man born to command.

He was, in truth, a born soldier, for he was the ideal height and weight, not too heavy for a trooper, and his muscles were like whipcord. His cheeks were bronzed and smooth, glowing with health, his nose was straight, and his mouth wide and good-natured. His chestnut hair was cropped short. He smiled easily, a reckless smile, when not in the midst of battle, as now, when his mouth was a straight, taut line.

His powerful chest was covered by a blue tunic, his curly hair by a cavalry Stetson strapped to his firm jaw. Cartridge belts crossed his body, supporting Colt revolvers. Blue whipcord trousers were tucked into fine black boots, with short-roweled spurs.

Hardened to peril, and utterly unafraid of the death that might face him at any moment, the Rio Kid was an ace fighting man.

He said nothing more to the captain, nor did the officer expect it. Captain Drew knew the Rio Kid, and there was no need for more words for a tacit understanding. If it were possible for any man to get through and bring aid—the Rio Kid would do it!

Pryor glanced toward the bunch of stamping, nervous horses, held by troopers in the scant protection of a small clump of cottonwoods. Many animals had gone down, their usefulness over, save as bulwarks. The order to kill

8

them all for this purpose had not yet been given, but the Rio Kid knew it would come soon.

Saber, his own horse, by which he set as great store as though the animal were human, was over there. The mount was a fleet-footed dun, so bad-tempered save with his own rider that others gave Saber a wide berth. He had a black stripe down his back, for he was of "the breed that never dies."

Saber did not fear gunfire. In fact, he would run toward it if not restrained. And in the excitement he would roll his mirled eye—an eye with blue and white streaks through the brown iris—as though the success of the encounter depended solely upon him. He was watching the Rio Kid now, restlessly, biting and threatening the other animals, for his uncanny animal instinct had told him even greater danger must soon be faced.

Two living things the Rio Kid loved above all others. One was this same Saber, and the thought of the dun's being sacrificed brought a lump to his throat.

"I can take him with me," he thought. "But—"

His eyes roved over the knoll, to settle on the second object of his affection and, looking, pain was poignant in his gaze. For long moments he stared at his trail companion, Celestino Mireles, a slim young Mexican whose life the Rio Kid once had saved on the Rio Grande. Since then an affection had grown up between the two that was a firm unbreakable tie.

The affection of Mireles, in truth, was more like worship. He would have followed the Rio Kid to the gates of the Inferno, and through.

Mireles' long, lean figure lay flat on the ground behind a hummock, the glinting rifle in his hand ready. The Rio Kid took in the familiar figure in a glance that might be his last—the young Mexican's hawk nose, the ink-black eyes and dark complexion. His wide sash flashed redly, and from it showed the hilt of the knife he so well knew how to use.

As if subconsciously aware of the steady stare, Mireles turned and nodded. He did not move. Fresh pain gripped the heart of the Rio Kid. Saber, he could take with him. But Mireles must be left behind. The young

9

Mexican's horse had been shot, none of the others could keep up with Saber, and on the dun's great speed depended the chance of survival of any of those valiant fighting troopers.

Celestino had guessed what was going on, that the captain had asked the Rio Kid to try a last, forlorn dash right through the Indian lines. And the kid knew that the Mexican was glad that his General, as he had always called the Rio Kid, would at least have a chance.

About him the Rio Kid saw his friends, men he knew and had been close to, lying dead or suffering agonies, without complaint. His jaw was set and a trickle of blood flowed from his bitten lip.

"Hullo, Bob!"

He turned quickly as a handsome corporal, whose stripes on his sleeve showed his rank, moved in nearer, grinning.

"How's it going, Billy?" asked Pryor.

Billy Lane, whom Pryor had known for some time at the Army post and on the move was a splendid young American, a good soldier. He was attempting a brave smile even now, while all about them the troopers were swearing, muttering in black fury, and with good cause. For metallic-looking objects sailed through the air like so many grasshoppers, as the soldiers discarded the cartridges.

"Look at these," Lane whispered, pushing a lot toward the Rio Kid.

Pryor picked up several. They looked like cartridges, but as he tried one with his nail, he found it was made of wood, a dummy. Some crooked contractor had made a million dollars supplying the Army—and the Rio Kid had the result before him.

"I'm goin' to ride to the Fort, Billy," he said. "Be back in a jiffy."

"You got plenty of nerve, Rio Kid." Young Lane shook his head. "I'd hate to try to ride through those—"

The shrieking, shooting red enemy had started in once more, and the Rio Kid snatched up his carbine. He would have to wait for a lull before trying his forlorn hope. Rifle slugs were buzzing over the trapped troopers now as thick as bees.

Corporal Billy Lane broke off his speech in the middle. He pulled trigger quickly, but the firing-pin clicked uselessly on a dud cartridge. Then he slumped by the Rio Kid and blood began pouring from his mouth.

"Lane—where'd yuh get it?" demanded Pryor, crouched beside his young friend.

"Neck—I—I—"

An Indian bullet had hit him over the collar-bone, and ranged down into his throat.

He could hardly speak, even whisper. The Rio Kid put his ear close to the moving lips to try to hear Billy Lane's dying words.

"My folks—Dakota—tell 'em—" A hand motioned weakly toward his tunic. "Take—"

Gently the Rio Kid took a picture from the tunic pocket. It showed Billy Lane with an older man who looked much like Billy, and a fine, middle-aged pioneer type of woman. On the other side stood a tall, smiling, beautiful girl.

"Yore sister, Billy? And yore father and mother?"

Lane nodded, but his eyes already were glazing. He was choking to death. As he drew his last breath, the Rio Kid's arm was beneath his young friend's shoulders. Slowly he rose, looking down at the dead young face.

With cold fury in his heart then, the Rio Kid started for the horses. Fury all the greater because he knew that with proper ammunition, the troopers would have driven the Indians off, though outnumbered ten to one. The savages did not like fighting against any number of seasoned troops in the open.

"Whoever supplied that junk," he muttered, "ought to have his hide took off in little pieces!"

The circling waves of braves had dashed in close, pouring lead into the diminishing band of soldiers. They rode almost to the rough breastworks before the deadly fire of what few guns held real cartridges discouraged them and they fell back.

Saber saw the Rio Kid coming and perked up. The Rio

11

Kid whistled a few bars of an old Army tune which Saber loved.

Said the big black charger to the little white mare.

Jerking his head hard, pulling his reins from the grip of the horse-holder, the dun broke away from the bunch and trotted to Pryor's side. Instantly the Army scout mounted.

With his pistols loaded with ammunition from his own belts, that he knew was good, and low over his mount, the Rio Kid dashed full-tilt after the breaking lines of the Sioux.

He was almost upon them before they realized his intention. Startled by the sheer madness of his move, they paused in astonishment. And in that breath of space the Rio Kid shot the two closest braves off their shaggy, bedecked ponies.

Fierce yells rose as he whirled on. Bullets hunted him. One burned through his hair, puncturing his Stetson, and another tore a hole in his tunic but did not bring blood. Zigzagging, he trusted the dun to hold a sure footing and run like the wind, while he swung in his leather, Colt up, and poured .45 slugs at the nearest of the deadly enemies riding full-tilt after him.

Indians were notoriously poor shots and, after the first couple of hundred yards, the Rio Kid knew he had a chance. Every long bound of the great dun made it more certain. If the horse did not hit a hole in the ground or a stray bullet catch up—

He switched to a fresh-loaded revolver. Behind him lay three Indians, while another had sprung from his falling horse, hit by the Rio Kid's fire.

Hoarse cheers came from the surviving soldiers. The Rio Kid made another hundred yards, while Indian braves began beating their mustangs to the pursuit. But though the fleet little Indian beasts could elude cavalry plugs, they could not match Saber. With the start he had, the Rio Kid pulled farther and farther ahead, while fifty raging Sioux stuck like weasels to his trail.

He killed a sub-chief who was in the van, and tore on

12

across the grassy, rolling waves of the land ocean. Direction meant nothing, for first he must get beyond gunshot. They forced him southeast, away from the direction of the Fort, where help lay. He would have to ride around, somehow, anyhow. He *must* save the remnants of the little force back there!

For an hour the Rio Kid drove on, always with the breath of red death at his neck. He had put enough space between himself and the Sioux not to worry much about a bullet, but dared not stop or they would be up for the kill.

Dust in the sky, its source hidden by one of the isolated prairie groves common to the region, turned him off to the southwest at a shallow angle. He was gambling, taking a fifty-fifty chance that he might run into white men, and not Indians.

He glanced back. The pursuers had seen this dust, too, and had dropped back a bit, to check it.

Then around the prairie grove rode two Indians. The Rio Kid cursed, pulled rein to evade the new band of savages. A gang of them appeared behind the two scouts riding in front, and shrill whoops reached his ears.

Then, astonishingly, and gratefully, he saw that the Sioux at his rear had turned tail. They were beating their mustangs, galloping them hard, back toward the main force surrounding the little band of troopers miles to the northwest.

He cursed, suddenly, with deep relief. A tall figure, a white man on a black stallion, cut from the prairie grove band and pounded his way, calling out. The Rio Kid swung the dun and hurried to meet him.

"Major North!" he cried, thrusting out his sweated, powder-stained hand to a man who was his friend.

Frank North, the "White Chief of the Pawnees," seized Pryor's hand, pumped it. They were close, with the ties of men who often had ridden together. North was a tall, thin soldier, with a clipped mustache and steady eyes. He was chief of several battalions of Pawnee Indians, hereditary enemies of the Sioux. To fight the Sioux, the Pawnees had thrown in their lot with the white men. North, with his red friends, who would follow him to the

13

death, had patroled the route of the trans-continental railroad while it was building, warding off the attacks of hostiles, guarding the work of gangs.

North had eighty seasoned fighters with him now, and they were at once in motion, heading for the battle scene.

When they reached the knoll where the Rio Kid had left his friends, the Sioux had fled. Dust in the sky showed the course of their retreat. They could not disguise the direction they had taken because it had been an exceptionally dry season and the grass was as dry as tinder. The rainfall had been scant, also, as it had been the year before.

The hostiles, warned by their own patrols that North and his redskins were approaching, had refused to stay and give battle. Long-distance shots were exchanged between the Pawnees and the Sioux, and the scouts kept up the pursuit for some miles, but real battle was over for the day.

Major North remained with the Rio Kid, looking on the awful death spot. There had been sixty troopers in the party under Captain Drew. Only twelve could walk to the horse lines.

Drew himself had been killed after the Rio Kid had made his bold dash through the heart of the enemy. Two lieutenants, three sergeants and seven corporals, among them Billy Lane, were dead. Seasoned, first-class cavalry troopers, every one a splendid fellow and a good soldier, as were the survivors.

The wounded must be tended, and the dead buried. Major North offered to have his Pawnee Battalion do this work.

The Rio Kid picked up several of the dud cartridges, which were responsible, chiefly, for the horrible death toll. He took them to Major North and mutely held them out. Mireles, Pryor's trail comrade, with one arm limp and a bloody crease in his cheek, stood silently by his friend.

North's face went angrily red as he glanced at the duds. He cursed, chewing at his mustache.

14

"Anybody who would pull such a trick should be made to pay, Rio Kid," he growled.

"He will," the Rio Kid promised grimly.

He went over to where the now dead sergeant had pried off the top of the box of dummy ammunition. There was no secret about where the duds had come from, whether the makers of the ammunition knew of them or not. For printed in black letters on the splintered box-top was the inscription:

SUNRISE ARMS AND AMMUNITION
COMPANY
ST. LOUIS, MO.

## CHAPTER II

## *Dusty Empire*

☐ Spruce and handsome, the Rio Kid pushed the dun across the rolling Dakota plain. His clothing and gear were as neat as anybody could have kept them in the blanket of dust that covered everything after those two dry years.

Even so, Bob Pryor looked almost as trim as he always did, in a new tunic, with freshly shined boots and Stetson cocked at a jaunty angle on his chestnut-haired head. His leather was oiled, well-tended. He had a passion for neatness, and during the campaigns of the Civil War he had learned how to keep himself in condition on the march. Saber, the dun, lifted his hoofs smartly despite the rolling dust and the heat of the summer sun.

Behind Pryor, on a beautiful, slim-limbed pinto, rode Celestino Mireles, his trail companion on the dangerous Frontier. The mount he rode had belonged to one of the dead soldiers. North had given the horse to the young Mexican. And Celestino's wounds had healed since the tragedy on the Niobrara when Captain Drew's troop had been all but wiped out due to the thieving greed of the contractor who had furnished the ammunition.

Investigators, hurrying to St. Louis, to arrest those responsible for the crime, had found the Sunrise Company closed. One Valentine Everts, head of the company, had fled. But it was believed that he could not long escape the vigilance of the government, because of his distinctive appearance. He was a man of good height but stooped, wore a thick black beard, and silver-rimmed spectacles. It was thought that he had crossed the Missouri, aware the Army police were after him, and had fled west for the Frontier. But all track of him had been lost. However, the Rio Kid had no intention of forgetting the matter, and the man's description was stamped indelibly on his brain.

Now he was carrying out the duty imposed on him by his dead friend, Billy Lane. He was seeking the young man's family to report to them personally, and to hand over Lane's effects. They had been notified of the soldier's death in battle through the regular channels, and the Rio Kid hoped that time would have dulled the first shock.

"Country looks like the devil—all dried out," he commented, as he and the Mexican rode along. "See that corn, Celestino? It's given up hope!"

The Rio Kid nodded toward a roughly ploughed field. The furrow tops were almost white, they were so crisply burnt, while the yellowish, dwarfed stalks were a travesty of healthy corn.

They topped a rise and could see down into a large, shallow valley through which ran a small stream. There was only a trickle of muddy water in the center, with a few tepid, brown pools here and there. The bed of the creek was parched and cracked.

"That must be it—Laneville," Pryor muttered.

Sod houses, built of thick chunks of prairie sod cut out and cemented together, with roofs of dirt laid on willow branches and canvas, showed here and there—pitiful little farms of settlers. A number of them clustered together as though for mutual protection, necessary in the land of the Sioux.

The field which the Rio Kid had noticed seemed typical of the surrounding farms. The drought had all these settlers by the throat.

Over all hung a coppery haze, the sun shining through

17

the fine, risen dirt. Some animals—cows and draught horses—stood in what shade the scrub trees along the stream offered.

The collection of soddies, with a couple of timber-built places, wood mostly imported by wagon or cut from green cottonwood that had shrunk, leaving big gaps, could hardly be called a town. It, and the surrounding farms, sheltered perhaps a dozen families, a hundred people at most.

A thin man, who looked young and yet sadly aged, stood at the shady end of a large sod-barn. He wore stained overalls and a straw hat and he was staring across the dreary plain as the Rio Kid rode up and politely greeted him.

"Howdy! Can yuh tell me where to find Norton Lane?"

The fellow's blue eyes turned slowly, but his expression did not change. He seemed to be in a state of permanent, mild shock.

"That's his house—the big one three houses down," he replied dully, then returned to his observation of nothing.

The Rio Kid rode on. He paused to let the dun and the pinto drink some muddy water from a trough fed by a wooden pipe from the creek, then sought the Lane home.

Dismounting, he dropped the dun's reins. The door in front stood open and he could look into the gloomy interior. Sun-blind, it took his eyes a few seconds to adjust themselves.

"Anybody home?" he called.

"Come in, stranger," a voice said.

A big man in a blue shirt and an old pair of jeans, his dark, fine head streaked with silver, had risen from a crude seat and stood looking at the Rio Kid. On the other side of the cold hearth sat a middle-aged woman with a patient, sweet face.

"Are you Norton Lane?" inquired Pryor.

"Yes, sir," the big man replied in his slow-spoken way.

In spite of all this man obviously had suffered, Bob Pryor still could see in his face something of eagerness and joy of life that had been in Corporal Billy Lane's face.

Billy Lane's father was bronzed to walnut hue by the sun. Lines of care had touched his once handsome face; his nose had a white scar on it, from some old injury. He had great hands, and the muscles in his brawny arms were strong and wiry. He had the vitality, a magnetic quality which Pryor had known in the son. His eyes, which never wavered, had a straightforward look.

"I was a friend of Billy's," the Rio Kid told Lane. "I promised him I'd come here and give yuh his things. I'm Bob Pryor."

Norton Lane stepped forward, his big hand out, and they shook.

The grim lines about the father's mouth tightened. The mother blinked, but held herself in well.

"You're very welcome here, sir," Lane said.

Alice Lane, Billy's young sister, came in from the kitchen lean-to then, wiping her hands on her calico apron. The Rio Kid had seen her picture, but his eyes widened as he saw her. The camera had not done her half justice.

She was tall, slim and graceful. Dark-brown hair, thick and wavy, fell to her shoulders. Her brown eyes were large and lustrous, her features molded into an unusual perfection of alluring sweetness. She was not more than seventeen or eighteen at most, the Rio Kid decided.

"This is my daughter Alice, Billy's sister," Norton Lane said gravely. "My wife, Sarah—Mr. Bob Pryor."

Women always looked twice at the debonair Rio Kid, with his good-humored, devil-may-care smile. These two did now, in spite of their grief. He bowed to Mrs. Lane, then turned to Alice.

She was too young, thought the Rio Kid, who had seen a good deal of such tragedy in his as yet short life, to be overcome by such a shock for long. Youth was always eager, always ready to forgive Fate and hope for the best. Otherwise, he had philosophically decided, life would not be worth its struggle for many.

"Good afternoon, Mr. Pryor," Alice said.

In her voice was a vibrant quality as pleasingly musical as the tones of a harp. It was the voice of a born singer, untrained, but naturally gifted. Unconsciously a

19

slim hand brushed a stray lock of hair into place—the unquenchable feminine desire to look well, especially before a personable young man.

In a short time the Rio Kid's presence enlivened the household. In fact, it seemed to awake the sun-dried town from its lethargy. People began appearing from the soddies and from the shady nooks they had sought to escape the sun. Men, women and children gravitated toward the Lane's home, staring at the visitors.

Mireles stayed outside, slouched on the ground with his bony shoulders hunched over, napping. The peaked sombrero shaded his face and he relaxed as he awaited the Rio Kid.

One of the first of the settlers to come in, at Lane's hearty welcoming call, was a large, strong young fellow in stained work jeans and shirt, and with a straw hat in one hand. He was in his early twenties, an eager-eyed, good looking bronzed farm worker. Stable boots covered his feet and shins, the overalls tucked inside.

"This is Dave Garrett, Rio Kid," Lane said, for Pryor had already mentioned the name by which he was so widely known.

Garrett was much interested in Bob Pryor, who was obviously a man of the world, and who would have news from the outside. He held out a powerful, calloused hand and showed even white teeth in a grin of welcome.

His face was open, easy to read; his earnestness was plain. His eyes were the blue of the prairie sky when it was behaving itself. He had rugged features, a good firm chin, a complexion that was a healthy pink under his sun-tan, and crisp light hair bleached by out-of-doors work.

"Howdy, sir," Garrett said. He spoke gravely, with a deliberate, measured accent.

His eyes turned upon Alice Lane, after he had stepped back from greeting the Rio Kid. As others came through the door at Norton Lane's call, Garrett gravitated toward Alice, and from the way she regarded him, Pryor decided the young farmer must be a suitor.

Pryor was busy shaking hands with the farmers. Most of them were a rugged, pioneering American type who had come westward to better their lot in life. There had been a depression after the Civil War and the restless trek had started men hunting new lands where they might bring up their families. The Sioux, however, had had something to say about this. They had hung on the outskirts of the settlements, making life dangerous, and Nature's vagaries had not helped these settlers any.

One of Norton Lane's older friends, Ben McCrory, impressed Pryor as an exceptional man. He was wide and strong of body, a blacksmith with brawny bare arms. He was not tall but made up for it in breadth and depth, and a chest like a hogshead showed through the open V of his worn flannel shirt. He had an open, infectious grin, and a cud of tobacco was thrust into one leathery, bearded cheek.

He roared a welcome and a quick jest to the Rio Kid. It was impossible not to smile in reply to McCrory's good humor.

Young fellows and their parents, girls and boys, smaller children, clustered about the Lane home, all gaping. Many of them looked peaked, and the Rio Kid realized they were not getting enough food.

The buffalo were being driven farther and farther west, and up to the north and south. Hide hunters were taking horrible toll of the tremendous and once apparently inexhaustible herds. The railroad had split the range and the beasts were growing shy at last, avoiding settlements and horsemen. So that the inhabitants of Laneville could not depend on a steady supply of such game.

"And it ain't even winter yet," thought the Rio Kid as, surreptitiously he studied the people who had come to greet him.

Many of them had a beaten, discouraged look, but there were few complaints. These were people who were used to hard times on the Frontier, who had learned that complaining was futile.

After a time, when he had shaken hands with fifty of the townsfolk, the Rio Kid gave more attention to individuals who had attracted him. The Green family, for instance, who had five small children, every one peaked and too thin. And the Corrigans, the Smiths, and others who were obviously in need of a helping hand.

When he at last was able to speak alone to Norton Lane, the Rio Kid gave the father the dead soldier son's last message of affection, and handed over Billy's effects.

The meal that was served by Alice and Mrs. Lane was proof of their poverty. It consisted of fried mush, sorghum molasses, a hunk of fat salt pork, and substitute coffee made of chicory. It was evidently a company dinner, too, because of the presence of Mireles and Pryor.

It was not long before the Rio Kid learned the story of the settlement's bad luck. The two years' drought had spoiled the crops, the earth, everything. Game animals had moved away, and the domestic creatures, prized for breeding and draught work, had had hard shift of it for water and proper herbage.

"It's been mighty bad," Norton Lane informed the Rio Kid, shaking his head. "I'll tell you, I've worried 'bout these folks, and what's to become of 'em."

"The Sioux bother yuh here, too, don't they?"

Yes, sir, they sure do. Last spring they shot Frank Sanders from ambush and carried off a little girl. We have to watch every second. They try to run off our horses and cattle, too, though lately they ain't been 'round so much. Busy in other parts, I reckon."

"Yuh ain't asked for my advice," the Rio Kid said, "but I'll offer it to yuh anyway, Mr. Lane. I hate to see folks like yore friends in this kind of trouble. I know this country. I've fought and scouted all over. Yuh picked a bad spot to settle in here and one that'll never grow easier. Fact is, I don't think yuh'll ever run long without drought, for it comes in spells. There's plenty of good land to be had."

Norton Lane stared at the Rio Kid's serious face.

"You mean—move?" he asked at last.

"That's what I mean. Yuh can't win here no matter how yuh try, so why stick with a losin' proposition? Go where the rainfall's surer and the land richer."

"But where?"

The Rio Kid hesitated, then replied:

"I picked up a copy of the Dodge City *Globe* a week

22

ago. It says that Ford County's open to dirt farmin', north of the Arkansas. The Texas drovers come up the Jones and Plummer now to Dodge, but they got to keep their cows south of the river. I been through there and the land's mighty fertile. It'll grow anything. Fact, I know the very valley where I'd settle if I was you."

A new light, one of fresh hope, shone in Norton Lane's eyes.

"By the eternal!" he cried, leaping to his feet and banging his fist on the table, "I believe you got the answer, Rio Kid! Wait'll I talk to the boys. We'd all oughta go, if one does."

The dusty dark had fallen over the plains. The warm evening breeze rustled the dry, curly buffalo grass, and stars showed in the murky sky. Small yellow patches of light shone from the dugout and soddy windows.

Norton Lane went out into the night and, seizing a large iron-headed mallet, struck a curved piece of railroad steel hanging from a crossbeam supported by two poles. The metal tone rang through the settlement, and men began emerging from their homes, rifles and shotguns in hand.

The Rio Kid, a cigarette glowing at his lips, had trailed Lane out, and stood watching.

"We ring our alarms when the Indians ride this way," exclaimed Lane. "It'll fetch 'em quick."

The settlers gathered at Lane's, and the big man raised his hand for silence. He explained the Rio Kid's plan, for them to move back east to Kansas.

"We've made a mistake and maybe lost three years, boys," Lane told them, "but we've had good experience and there's no use to be bull-headed. Let's admit we were wrong to come here, and start fresh where the Rio Kid says to. I'm convinced. How many agree?"

Hands started to rise. Some hesitated, but joined in as more and more voted to leave. Only a few refused to vote for the shift.

Hope came again into many a dull eye that night. Plans were set on foot for a trek to new lands.

# CHAPTER III

## *The Cowboy Capital*

☐ A drunkard staggered down the aisle of a train rolling across the plains westward, and slumped into a seat. The conductor approached.

"Ticket, please?"

"No ticket!"

"Where you want to go?" demanded the trainman.

"To hell!"

"Okay. Four dollars, please—and get off at Dodge City."

The Rio Kid had heard this yarn, and had heard others of the wild ways and fighting in Dodge. He had passed through the town but had never spent much time there. But lately Dodge had roared up into such a mad, fierce life that no frontiersman could resist its lure. Nor was the Rio Kid an exception. He wanted to see and learn more of Dodge City.

The town lay near the bend of the Arkansas River in southwest Kansas. It was in the heart of the buffalo country, and bearded, hard-eyed hunters stalked the streets, trading in skins and meat.

Piles of buffalo bones as high as hotels lined the railroad tracks and miles on miles of cattle pens were strung down the Santa Fe right-of-way. Bellowing never ceased, night or day, from these tens of thousands of throats, while in the darkness the campfires of Texas cowmen, squatting sometimes for months on the prairie to fatten their beeves for sale after the hard drive up from the Lone Star State, flickered like so many beacons.

Dodge City had become the Mecca of all those who dwelt in the West, of the buffalo men, the drovers, gunmen, gun-fighters, gamblers, the women who followed them, and of men who sought business with Dodge citizens, either above-board or shady. There had been cowtowns before but none as big and wild as Dodge. The annual cattle drive had swollen until half a million head came up the Jones and Plummer Trail, to seek market.

The Rio Kid, followed by the faithful Celestino Mireles, stared curiously as he approached from the southwest over the Toll Bridge across the river. The town had grown in leaps and bounds since his last visit here.

South of the railroad were low dives, saloons and gambling houses. There was the rough part of the settlement. North of the tracks, Dodge was more or less respectable.

The two comrades crossed the tracks and swung onto Front Street, the main thoroughfare, a wide, dusty road that ran east and west, north of the railroad. Bridge Street, which they had followed up from the river, was the chief north and south way.

Front Street widened out into a plaza, with saloons and stores around the three upper sides of the square. The station, water tanks and other railroad buildings were near at hand. Large hotels and drinking oases were everywhere, as well as stores advertising their various wares.

The Rio Kid and Celestino drank in the sights. The streets were crowded with buffalo hunters in buckskin, with Texas cowboys stalking in bowlegged stride from saloon to saloon, guns prominent, spurs jingling. There were dark-clad, sleek gamblers, and young women with painted cheeks and rouged lips.

Saddle horses stood by the hundreds at the rails. Wagons, buckboards and freighters, every sort of vehicle, filled every available spot. Music came from a number of places, combining, with the shouts of teamsters, the distant bellowing of cattle, the far-off rumble of a train and other sounds into a mad medley.

Dodge, on the Kansas prairie, was dust and heat, and quivering with barbaric force.

"Hey there, Rio Kid!"

A man standing on the curb in the shade of an awning sang out a greeting, and Bob Pryor turned Saber's head in. He grinned broadly.

"Bat! How are yuh?"

The Rio Kid dismounted and ducked under the rail, thrusting out a hand to the smiling young fellow who had greeted him—Bat Masterson who had already made a name for himself throughout the West. He and the Rio Kid were friends, having worked together many times.

Masterson was as lithe as a panther, a true frontiersman and gun-fighter. His blue eyes with their flickers of jade green were marble-hard, and he wore a corn-colored mustache. Quick of eye, steady of hand and a master with firearms, Bat Masterson's already was a name to conjure with on the Frontier.

Bat had an artistic streak, and his clothing was showily splendid. His sombrero was circled by a gold bullion band worked into the shape of a rattler, with red glass eyes. A crimson sash decorated his lean waist—but there was nothing fancy about the businesslike pistols that rode it. A star was pinned to the lapel of his open vest— a sheriff's star.

"C'mon into Kelley and Beatty's Alhambra and have a drink with me," Masterson invited, slapping the Rio Kid on the back.

As they swung to enter the big saloon, a genteel-looking man with a long, hawklike nose and crisp black mustache nearly ran into Masterson. His piercing black eyes glinted with ironic humor as he bowed with mock respect to the officer.

"Oh, I beg yore pardon, Sheriff Masterson," he said in an evenly sarcastic voice. "My error."

He wore cowboy rig, with a Stetson strapped over his curling black hair, leather chaps to protect his trousers from constant friction with a saddle, an open vest, and fine boots with silver spurs. A belt filled with .45 cartridges supported two supple holsters in which rested his Colts.

But Masterson's cold eyes fixed the fellow.

"Check yore guns in town, Henry," the sheriff said.

"Sorry. I'm just leavin'. Is that all right?"

Bat Masterson nodded. He waited while the man he had called Henry walked around himself and the Rio Kid with exaggerated care, ducked under the hitch-rack and went to a beautiful, long-limbed black which plainly was of the best Arabian strain. Horseflesh was a matter of first importance on the Frontier, and the Rio Kid and Bat Masterson knew that the animal was worth five, six, or seven hundred dollars—anything the owner could get.

Henry mounted with the ease of a born rider and trotted off down the dusty way.

"I'll kill that son one day," Masterson said dispassionately, and spat into the gutter.

"Who is it?" asked Pryor.

"That's Dutch Henry, the biggest hoss thief in the West. He steals 'em from the Rio to Montana. As many as three hundred outlaws run with him and his pard Tom Owens when he gives the call."

"If he's a hoss thief, why don't yuh arrest him?"

"I have," replied Masterson, stepping aside to let the Rio Kid enter the brightly-lighted saloon first. "So have a dozen other sheriffs. But he always gets out of it. Bribes witnesses or scares 'em and fools the judges. He's too clever to pull a gun when it's anyways near even."

They crossed the sawdust-covered expanse of the saloon floor. Music came from the rear, and gamblers were busy. Behind the long bar with gilt-edged mirrors and every modern convenience, were half a dozen tenders.

Masterson was greeted cheerfully as he approached the bar. Everybody knew Bat Masterson, and all except criminal characters liked him and respected his integrity, as well as his speed with a Colt. No better peace officer existed. He knew exactly how to handle the egotistical, drink-maddened gunmen of the Frontier.

A big, heavy man with a walrus mustache and a grin on his seamed face, got up from a table and strolled over to Masterson and the Rio Kid. He slapped Bat on the back.

"Hullo, my boy. Glad to see yuh so . . . By jumpin' horntoads if it ain't the Rio Kid!"

"Howdy, Kelley," Pryor said, smiling as he shook hands.

James "Dog" Kelley had been in the Army at one time, in fact had been an orderly to General George Custer, and the Rio Kid, one of Custer's officers himself, was acquainted with him. But it was since his Army days that Kelley had acquired his nickname. He loved hunting, and used big greyhounds to run game on the Plains, some of which Custer had presented to him. He was popular in Dodge, an early resident, and half-owner of the huge saloon in which they stood.

"Yuh can't pay for drinks in here," Kelley said, as the Rio Kid reached for money after the second drink. "What fetches yuh to these parts, Pryor?"

"Mebbe yuh can help me about that," the Rio Kid suggested. "I'm on the trail of a sidewinder named Valentine Everts, a hombre with a thick beard and silver-rimmed specs. Think mebbe he headed for these parts. He cheated the Army by unloadin' a passel of fake cartridges on 'em and—"

He gave a quick picture of the fight in which the troopers had died, trying to hold off the Sioux with duds.

Dog Kelley whistled. "A skunk that would do a thing like that," he growled, "deserves Indian torture 'fore he gets the bullet that's comin' to him. What makes yuh think he headed for Dodge?"

The Rio Kid shrugged. "A hunch, that's all. He came West, and I figured this was the place to ask for him. Sooner or later every shady devil on the Frontier'll hit Dodge."

"That's the truth," agreed Bat Masterson. "There's plenty of 'em here now."

Dog Kelley nodded gravely. "Bat's right. Town's full of wild men, Rio Kid. I'll ask around for this—Everts, yuh say his name was?"

"Yeah, Val Everts."

Kelley nodded, left them to their drinks, and started to circulate through the saloon. Now and then he would pause to put his big hand on a man's shoulder or to buy a cowboy a drink. He would speak with the man, and the Rio Kid guessed he was seeking information about the criminal contractor.

"He's a good man," Masterson remarked, nodding toward Kelley. "Too good-hearted, for a fact. There's an election comin' up—we're right in the middle of it, Rio Kid—and Dog's goin' to have his hands full with it. Yuh can't see it, but it's a fight 'tween the good and the bad for control of Dodge. Oh, don't get the notion that Dog is growin' little white wings, for he ain't. He's willin' to let gamblin' and liquor have their fling, but it's got to be done in a halfway decent manner."

A tall, pleasant-faced young man in corduroy pants, a blue shirt, and with a dark Stetson topping his handsome head, strolled in and paused beside them, grinning.

"Know my brother Ed?" inquired Bat.

"Howdy!" cried the Rio Kid, shaking hands heartily. "Shore great to know yore brother, Bat."

Ed Masterson was a good-natured, splendid youth. But his character was not so sharply etched as that of his elder brother.

The Rio Kid and the two Mastersons had a drink, and Bob Pryor learned that many of his Frontier friends were in town. Texas drovers and buffalo hunters were as thick as fleas around Dodge, and soldiers from nearby Fort Dodge, on the Arkansas River, helped keep things humming for the Northern marshals who sought to maintain a semblance of order.

Ed Masterson finally took his leave and went outside. And after a time Dog Kelley came back.

"No luck yet on that Everts skunk, Rio Kid," he informed. "But I'll keep askin' and we'll track him. Everybody of his brand hits Dodge one time or another, like Bat here said. Or some of his pards will let slip where he's hidin'."

"Thanks," Pryor said.

Masterson emptied his glass.

"I better make the rounds, Rio Kid. Have to patrol regular-like, yuh know. By the way, Wyatt Earp's over on the west side of the plaza."

"I'll step along with yuh," the Rio Kid said promptly. "I'll be right glad to see Wyatt."

They strolled from Kelley's Alhambra Saloon, Gambling Hall and Restaurant and took to the crowded sidewalks. Dark had fallen and the town was beginning to warm up for the night. It was a great spot, and merrymakers were starting to howl for the evening.

# CHAPTER IV

## *Drygulched*

☐ Celestino Mireles took charge of the horses, Saber and his own, while the Rio Kid went along with Bat Masterson.

"What's the law on homesteadin' in these parts, Bat?" asked the Rio Kid, as they walked.

"Farmers? There's a new agreement, Rio Kid, 'tween the grangers and cowmen—there's always trouble when they try to mix trail herds and growin' crops, yuh savvy. The law says that settlers must stay north of the Arkansas River. This gives the drovers a chance to fetch their steers to Dodge up the Jones and Plummer without runnin' over planted fields."

The Rio Kid nodded. "That's what I heard, Bat."

Masterson's eyes twinkled as he looked sideward at the debonair gunfighter by him. "Yuh thinkin' of tryin' yore hand at farmin'?"

The Rio Kid grinned. "Not yet, Bat. Not till I'm ninety, anyway. I brought some folks over here from the Dakota country to settle and planted 'em in the low hills forty miles west of here. It's north of the river, as that's what I understood it must be. They're in temporary camp and I came in to arrange for 'em to buy food to run 'em through the winter months. They were in a bad way out where they was in Dakota."

"I savvy. Well, Kansas is glad to have 'em. If they're friends of yores they'll stack up."

At the corner, Bat Masterson paused to speak to a dark-faced, black-haired, stocky man wearing a town marshal's badge.

"Yuh know Neal Brown?" Bat asked the Rio Kid.

Neal Brown, a Cherokee breed, turned quick black eyes to the Rio Kid, shook hands. Brown never had much to say but he was a first-class fighting man and a fine peace officer of Dodge.

After a moment's conversation, Masterson and the Rio Kid went on, entering several of the bigger saloons. Bat Masterson assisted the Rio Kid in his inquiries concerning Valentine Everts, the crooked contractor whom Pryor was determined to bring to justice.

The evening wore on, and Dodge grew noisier and more blatant as liquor inflamed tempers. The Rio Kid saw one old acquaintance after another.

One acquaintance, Ben Thompson, was playing in a bright spot. He was a tall man with a flowing dark mustache, and no deadlier marksman with shotgun and Colt ran the Frontier. He winked and grinned at Bob Pryor, who had tangled with the famous gambler on more than one occasion. Thompson held no hard feelings.

Aware that Thompson knew everything about everybody in the wild places of the West, shady or otherwise, the Rio Kid waited an opportunity. When a hand had just been finished and Thompson had raked in the pot, he spoke to the gambler.

"I'm huntin' a hombre named Valentine Everts, Thompson," the Rio Kid said in a lowered tone.

The other five men at the table stared at him, with ill-veiled impatience to get on with their game.

"I never heard of him," Thompson replied, rather coldly.

Patiently the Rio Kid started to explain, for he wanted Thompson to understand that this was not a personal feud. He was sure that there could be no man with a soul in him who would not want the contractor to pay for what he had done. While he was explaining, however, a young fellow with wavy, ash-blond hair, and a thin, haggard face, turned deep-set blue eyes angrily up to the Rio Kid.

Pryor's glance swept that face in a quick, all-inclusive look—the neatly trimmed mustache, the fine nose, the expressive but deadly mouth.

"We're busy, sir," the man snarled. "Would you mind removing your carcass from—" He broke into a fit of coughing.

"Sorry," drawled the Rio Kid, eyes narrowing a bit. "This is mighty important."

The blond young gambler pushed back his chair with a swift fury, jumping to his feet to face the Rio Kid.

"Hey, Doc, take it easy, will yuh?" protested Ben Thompson.

The Rio Kid and the man called "Doc" eyed one another like a pair of hostile dogs about to tangle. Blood boiled to fever heat in an instant in Dodge, when such men were involved. Everybody knew that guns would bark at any moment.

The Rio Kid was not hunting trouble, but he was not a man to run away from it either. His blue eyes pinned the cold orbs of the blond gambler facing him.

"Get the devil—" Doc had started to say, when a tall man hastily entered the saloon and sang out:

"Oh, Doc! Meet my friend the Rio Kid!"

It was Chief Marshal Wyatt Earp, on duty in Dodge, who had entered. The leonine, powerful and rangy marshal came over to the table as Doc and the Rio Kid paused. Earp was a striking figure in dark pants and shirt, and a black Stetson that shaded his face with its tawny mustache and deep-set eyes.

As the Rio Kid knew, he was about the greatest of peace officers known. Two long-nosed Colts in his holsters emphasized his calling.

Earp had a genius for being on hand when trouble started. He had just met Bat Masterson on the street, who had told him the Rio Kid was in town. Entering this saloon to say howdy to his friend Pryor, Earp had taken in the scene and instantly diagnosed it.

"This is Doc Holliday, a pard of mine, Pryor," Earp said heartily. "Doc, shake hands with the Rio Kid, one of the best."

The Rio Kid pricked up his ears. So this was Doc Holliday! He had heard of the tubercular gambler, of his deadly guns and vile temper. The man's slender fingers could draw and fire a six-shooter with astounding speed and he was a man of ice.

Wyatt Earp, however, as was generally known held a powerful influence for good over Doc Holliday. Holliday's complete loyalty and affection for the great peace officer was, perhaps, the gambler's only redeeming feature. It was a strange friendship, the murderous, deadly gunman and gambler on one side, the cool, masterful marshal on the other. Doc had once saved Earp's life in a pinch and they had been friends ever since.

"Glad to know you, Rio Kid," Holliday said. He lapsed into another violent coughing fit and then sat down. The players and the marshal listened then while Pryor told of his hunt for Valentine Everts. No one knew a man of that name and the description the Rio Kid could give was hardly full.

"My luck's out," a small, alert man remarked, pushing back his chair, "I'm quittin'."

"Okay, Frenchy," Ben Thompson said.

"Frenchy" Dupuy, as he had been introduced to the Rio Kid, cashed in what few chips he had. He was a slender, short fellow, with tight curly black hair, a spot goatee under his curving lower lip, a crisp little mustache on his upper. He had large, long-lashed violet eyes and a slender, high-bridged nose. He wore a full-fashioned frock coat, pearl-gray trousers tight about his legs and polished calfskin boots. His hat was black, with a narrow brim. A thick gold watch chain adorned his fancy checked vest.

"Come along," he said, clapping the Rio Kid on the back. "I'll buy a drink." He was quick to smile, showing even, small white teeth. "You have cut yourself a task, my friend. Such a devil as this Everts you describe should be punished. But the Frontier is large. What will you do when you come up with him—that is, if you have the luck?"

The Rio Kid shrugged. "That depends on what *he* does, Dupuy. I hope he don't choose to answer to the law. In that case it'll be man to man."

Dupuy studied the Rio Kid for a time. Then he nodded.

"He deserves that you track him down!"

Dupuy had a great deal of magnetism. He had an ingratiating manner and a genius for pleasing others. The Rio Kid enjoyed the little fellow's talk and constant jests.

Half an hour later he went outside and kept on through the hot spots of Dodge. The town was roaring full-speed ahead by midnight and there had been several fights in the plaza, which were quickly broken up by the veteran and skillful marshals.

Finally the Rio Kid stepped from a smoke-filled, noisy saloon, and ducked under the hitch-rack to cross to the plaza and get a breath of fresh air. He was getting tired, for he usually went to bed early.

Mireles was over at the Crown Livery Stable, sleeping in the hay near the horses, and Pryor decided to join his comrade. Just as he swung away, however, a bullet tore a gash in his left arm, puncturing the flesh three inches above his elbow.

He fell to his knees in the dusty street and though the shock of the wound was great, he made a flash draw that was so fast his hand was only a blur. The shot had come from behind him, a cowardly drygulcher's bullet. It had missed as he had changed his direction, cut his arm instead of driving through under his shoulder-blade to the heart.

A second bullet whined over his head and he caught the flash of the rifle from a dark alleyway, a narrow path separating two big gambling establishments on Front Street. He replied at once, Colt barking, and the skulking opponent did not shoot again.

Leaping up, with blood pouring from his wound, and tingling sensations running down his injured arm, the Rio Kid dived toward the spot in which he had located

35

his attacker, his pistol blaring. Reaching the alley, he heard retreating footsteps and followed at full speed, revolver cocked under his thumb.

A dark figure—the man who had made the attempt on Pryor's life running away—passed a light streak from a window. The Rio Kid, whose reflexes were fast as flashes of lightning, shot again. The fellow went down, crashing hard on his face.

Shouts of alarm rose behind him. The shooting had attracted attention and city marshals were hurriedly converging on the scene.

Wyatt Earp was first to reach the Rio Kid's side. The tall marshal ran up, to find Pryor bending down, a lighted match in his hand, studying the evil face of a dead man on the ground.

"What the devil happened?" demanded Earp.

Bob Pryor quickly told him. The blood on his sleeve showed that there had been a duel, and the short-barreled carbine close beside the dead man had been fired three times.

Bat Masterson, Neal Brown and another marshal raced in then. Bat stared down at the burly, bearded man on the ground. The dead man's range clothing was nondescript—cowboy pants, vest and shirt, and a Stetson strapped to his greasy head. His face was evil, and his beard did not altogether conceal the ugly pockmarks that pitted it.

"One-Finger Keely," growled Bat. In a lower voice, to the Rio Kid, he said, "He's a pard of Dutch Henry's. Watch yore step. Yuh got any idea why they'd go after yuh?"

Pryor shook his head. "It's a mystery to me, Bat. I've only been in town a few hours."

He went along with his friends to the City Hall, where his wound was dressed.

# CHAPTER V

## *Kill Order*

☐ George Frenchy Dupuy turned the knob of the door to the rear room of a small house set between others on Dodge's South Side, across the Santa Fe tracks.

The hot smell of burning oil, mingling with whiskey, greeted his widened nostrils. There was a cot on one side of the square room, a table which held the remains of a meal, a bottle of whiskey and a glass, tobacco and pipe, a newspaper. Clothing hung from hooks screwed into the board wall.

A man looked up and nodded as Dupuy entered and carefully shut the door after him.

"Hello, Frenchy," the man said.

He had a hoarse, unpleasant voice. His frame was bony, and long legs were stretched out before him. His face was rapacious, with a heavily-lined, thin-lipped mouth that turned down at the corners. His chin came to a small but bulging point. He wore no beard or mustache and his hair was a faded brown with light streaks through it. His keen gray eyes held a suspicious gleam.

Frenchy Dupuy pulled up a chair, poured himself a drink and downed it slowly, while the man who had been waiting watched him curiously.

"There's a man in town lookin' for you, Everts," Dupuy said then in a silky voice.

Val Everts scowled. "I see. Who is he, and what's his game, Frenchy?"

Dupuy did not meet Everts' gaze for a moment but stared into the ruby depths of the whiskey in his glass. Then he began:

"His name's the Rio Kid. He was in an Indian fight with a patrol of the Fourth Cavalry on the Niobrara when the Sioux hit 'em. Most of the troopers died and it impressed him—especially the ammunition, which wouldn't go off. The Rio Kid took the trouble to check up and found it had come from the Sunrise Arms Company. Do you savvy?"

Everts leaped to his feet with a furious oath, eyes flaming.

"Get rid of him!" he snarled.

"I've already tried."

"Well?"

"I had a friend of ours sic One-Finger Keely on him about half an hour ago. Keely's dead."

"So this Rio Kid's that kind, is he?"

"Quick as a flash, and an ace shot. They all know him —Masterson and Earp—and it's said he's one of the gamest gun-fighters on the Frontier. He ain't what you could call a cinch."

"Huh. If Keely missed him and he downed One-Finger, he must be good. No dirtier drygulcher ever skulked a dark alley than Keely. It wasn't luck?"

"Nope. He hit Keely after One-Finger's first bullet tore his arm. That rattled Keely and the Rio Kid got him through the heart when Keely turned to run."

Everts resumed his seat, a crafty gleam replacing his first rage.

"So his game is to bring the Sunrise Arms to justice, eh?"

"That's it. Oh, you're safe enough for the moment, Boss. You've dyed your hair and shaved off the beard you grew, and got rid of the cheaters you wore back in St. Loo. But I've asked around and this Rio Kid is dynamite. He'll never quit."

Deep lines corrugated Val Everts' pasty brow. Not only had he changed his appearance, but he had changed his name. He was known in Dodge as Phillip Harrison. The money he had obtained by selling dummy ammunition which had meant the sacrifice of the lives of his country's soldiers had enabled him to buy in at Dodge. He had certain ambitions he wished to realize.

"Yes, Dupuy, you're right," he agreed at last. "Such a fellow's too dangerous. If he came up with me it'd ruin my game in Dodge just when I've started. Where's he livin'?"

Dupuy made an expressive gesture with his fine, slim hands.

"I'm no magician, Boss. After all, I just bumped into him tonight, got onto him when he inquired around town for you. He likes me, and we had a couple drinks together. I'll keep an eye on him. That sort doesn't generally have any set home. They sleep where their horse happens to be. The Rio Kid's is at the Crown Livery."

"Huh. One man can't check me. But I can't stand any publicity about the past."

Everts got up and paced restlessly about the smoke-filled room, his long muscles flowing like a stalking panther. After a while he turned again to Frenchy Dupuy.

"Go next door to the Blue Buffalo and tell Dutch Henry I want him," he ordered.

Frenchy nodded and slipped·out the back way. Presently he returned with the good-looking Henry, whose piercing black eyes shone with sardonic humor.

"Siddown and have a drink, Dutch," Everts growled.

The horse-thief chieftain nodded, and took the chair close to Everts.

"Now look here," Everts began. "You still haven't any love for Masterson, Earp, Kelley and their crew, have you?"

Dutch Henry shrugged. "Yuh know I ain't. They're always persecutin' me."

"We had a little talk last week and you promised to back me. When I'm mayor of Dodge I'll fire those skunks and run Masterson out of·the town, sheriff or not. I'll ap-

39

point you chief marshal and you can pick your own assistants. There's a million in it."

"I'm with yuh. I've lined up a bunch of votes."

"Somethin's come up. A hombre they call the Rio Kid just pulled into town and—well, I can't have him around. Get rid of him for me."

Dutch Henry's eyes opened a bit.

"The Rio Kid? I savvy him. That was him with Bat Masterson tonight, wasn't it?"

"Yeah, that's the man," Frenchy Dupuy said. "He just downed One-Finger Keely."

The horse thief swore. He had been gambling south of the tracks and the rumpus had not penetrated beyond the deadline, as the Santa Fe railroad was called.

"Keely was a pard of mine," he snapped. He rose. "I'll check this Rio Kid up," he said shortly.

"Watch him, though. He's quick."

"Yuh don't need to tell me."

"He's turned in over at the Crown Livery. His death'll embarrass Masterson and Earp and Kelley. We can use it as a campaign point—that they can't maintain order and prevent murders."

"All right."

Dutch Henry strode out.

The Rio Kid had hardly fallen asleep, rolled in his blanket near the stall where Saber was kept, when he came awake once more.

The slight click of a half-door being opened, close to him, had roused his alert senses, trained to danger. Dodge City was howling at full-roar in the night, but only the immediate threat to himself caused Pryor to wake.

The scar on his left side, a memento from Gettysburg, a wound taken there, itched violently. That was a sure warning of peril. His hand was already closing on the butt of his Colt revolver, never far from it.

He heard a faint whisper:

"It's dark as cats in here—can't see nothin'."

The faint block of light where the open door was became shadowed by several hatted figures.

"Strike a match," someone ordered hoarsely. "He's snorin' by this time."

Not to disappoint them, the Rio Kid gave several snores. At once they turned his way and he caught the glint of light on rising gun barrels. He guessed these men might be a party come to revenge One-Finger Keely. Such a man would have plenty of shady friends.

A match flared, and a covered bull's-eye lantern was hastily lit, the beam shaded under a coat.

"This way, boys," the leader whispered. "Wait'll we make shore it's him."

They wore cowboy Stetsons, and all had guns. Behind the bulge of the thick beam, the Rio Kid waited, curious to see if this was meant to be a finish-up of the Keely affair. On tiptoe, a dozen men came inside, two in front, the others trailing. And outside there seemed to be more, and the dark shapes of horses were visible through the opening.

"Lookin' for somebody?" the Rio Kid inquired suddenly.

They checked, blinked. The bull's-eye beam came toward them.

"Say, do yuh know a feller named the Rio Kid?" asked the leader. "Some friends of his are lookin' for him."

"Why, that's me," Pryor answered. "What's up, boys?"

"C'mon over and have a drink. Bat wants yuh."

"I don't feel in the mood. Anyhow, I just left Bat."

They were sifting around into position, to get a clear bead on him. "Aw, be a sport, Rio Kid," the burly, bearded gunman growled. "Just one swaller."

"Not even a sniff, gents. I'm plumb wore out. Dust, and let me sleep."

One of them opened the ball, impatient for glory and to have it over with. He fired from the hip, the bullet cutting a big splinter from the beam. On the echo the Rio Kid's Colt roared and the gunman doubled up and fell in the straw.

The bull's-eye was dropped, and went out. All shifted position, Colts and shotguns exploding in a deafening volley that filled the stable until the horses were snorting and stamping in fright.

Lead bit into wood, shrieked in the dark air. The Rio Kid was back against the wall, Colt in hand, and he shot at the flashes of his foes' weapons. A cursing shout told he had made a hit, and a heavy thud meant a man down. In the blue-yellow flares the battle could be momentarily glimpsed.

"Get in here, blast yuh!" bellowed the gunmen's chief.

There was a rush of men through the door and from several angles came lead hunting for the Rio Kid, nestled in his niche of wood. He kept the direct line clear of them with his accurate pistol.

"Come on, boys!" he heard the leader shout. "There ain't much time left!"

He picked up a second revolver to shoot with both hands when they piled in on him. Heavy boots shook the rickety flooring and the stable was filled with gun sound.

To slow them, the Rio Kid fired, swiftly, revolvers moving in a semicircle, bullets tearing into flesh and bone, for there were so many crowded together, that he could hardly miss. If they were willing to lose a few men, they could kill him. He could not keep such a mob off in the dark for long.

It was a desperate moment. There was no way out. The nearest window was past the stalls and he was cornered. Cool as a cucumber, the Rio Kid prepared to take as many as he could with him.

"In and finish him!" shrieked the chief gunny.

They had started the rush and he was crouched down behind his beam, ripping them with lead, but aware that only instants of life remained, when a call came from outside. It slowed them.

"Here they come!" the horse-holder outside shouted through the door.

Sulphurous profanity mingled with the burnt-powder fumes. The warning was urgent and the mob of gunmen paused. The Rio Kid made good use of his chance. More shouts went up, and then, with a final burst of lead, they turned and made for the door.

"Halt!" a stentorian voice yelled from the street, and gunshots rang out.

They answered the shots, leaping for their saddles.

The Rio Kid sprang to his feet, and jumped the still quivering corpse of a killer he had just sent to perdition. He made for the open door, to help the others on their way with bullets, his fighting blood boiling.

Down the alley from the street came a running group of Dodge City men. Wyatt Earp's tall figure was in the van, and Bat Masterson's voice was ordering the gang to wait and have it out.

But they had had plenty. They would not face the quick-shot marshals. Inside of seconds they had spurred around the stable and were pounding away along Tin Can Alley.

Mireles, Earp, Masterson, Brown and three other men came dashing up, guns ready. But the battle was over.

A lantern was lighted. Inside lay three dead killers. Bat Masterson looked them over curiously.

"H'm. I know that one, boys. He's said to have traveled with Dutch Henry's gang."

"He won't travel any more," remarked Earp.

Celestino Mireles had brought help. He had been asleep on the other side of the big stable when the fight had started, and had slid out a window and given Masterson the alarm. Bat was furious and so was Earp.

"The dogs!" Bat growled. "They come to even it up on account of Keely, I reckon. Rio Kid, we'll stand guard for yuh. You git some shut-eye. Yuh need it."

The Rio Kid was glad to take advantage of Bat's kind offer.

He turned in again and slept through the night, undisturbed by the wicked howl of Dodge, the Babylon of the Plains.

# CHAPTER VI

## *New Arrivals*

☐ David Garrett, the reins of his four-horse team in big, work-calloused hands, felt deep inner happiness as he looked at the rosy-cheeked, smiling girl who sat on the wide seat beside him.

He knew that he was in love with her and that she was the girl for him. To a man of his constant nature and even temperament there could never be any other.

The trek from arid Sioux land to Kansas had been stimulating and exciting for the younger members of Norton Lane's community. Garrett had no family and had proved a tremendous pillar of strength for the weaker settlers, the old ones, and the children. He was always ready to help anybody in distress.

Large and powerful, his blue eyes deep and steady, Garrett was the kind of man who could be depended upon to the end. And he wore his worn farmer clothing proudly.

The girl, Alice Lane, was more volatile. Tall and with the strength that pioneer blood gives, the pretty girl enjoyed gaiety. Her big brown eyes sparkled now, because of the crisp beauty of the autumn morning. She was wearing her best calico dress and blue sunbonnet, while a buffalo robe kept her warm.

44

"Oh, it's wonderful, isn't it, David?" she exclaimed.

"Yes, mighty nice," he agreed, smiling. Anywhere she was would be wonderful for him, he thought.

Behind Garrett's wagon came Norton Lane's. His wife was with him and several other women of the new camp west and north of Dodge had come along. Sixteen big vehicles were in the line, headed toward Dodge City to get supplies for the coming winter. They had brought some seed along and their tools and work animals, but not before the next late summer could any crops be harvested and sold. Cash was scarce.

"I hope the Rio Kid savvied what he was talkin' about," Garrett remarked, "when he guaranteed he'd get us credit in Dodge, Alice."

The girl stopped smiling, and looked at him sharply.

"He said he would, didn't he? When Bob Pryor says anything you can bet it's so."

Garrett had not meant to doubt their friend, who had taken such a deep interest in their fate. Alice's quick defense of the Rio Kid, however, roused a spark in him that he couldn't put out. It was jealousy, the primeval emotion ever present in a man where his mate is concerned.

But ever since the Rio Kid had put in an appearance, Alice had admired him. Garrett liked Bob Pryor, but he was beginning to grow uneasy. The girl was always talking about the dashing Rio Kid.

Garrett knew he could not match Pryor at gun fighting, at the wild life he led, could never equal the Rio Kid's gallantry and background. He was a plain farmer; not an adventurer. But above everything, he wanted to win Alice Lane.

It was necessary for the new settlers to get to town and file on their sections, as well. After paying the Government charge and filing, they must build houses within a certain period and start improvement in order to establish full title.

The sight of Dodge, the greatest of Frontier towns and of which all had heard so many wicked tales, thrilled Alice Lane and her friends. They whipped up the horses and rattled into the settlement at a smart pace, dust rising under the heavy wheels.

"Oh, there's the Rio Kid!" cried Alice, jumping up and waving frantically to a horseman who was coming across the plaza toward them.

Garrett pulled up his wagon at the side of the dusty street. The town was full of cowboys, while long-haired buffalo hunters, lean and fierce, Indians with painted faces and blankets, gamblers in black broadcloth and straight hats, and other Frontier denizens wandered about. Stores and saloons were wide open and over the South Side hung a hazy smoke pall.

Out on the plains around the city were blanket camps, where Texas men held their steers, driven up the Jones and Plummer from the Lone Star State. Garrett told Alice about them, and explained how sometimes the beeves would be fattened on the prairie grass for months before finally being disposed of for market. When they lost weight on the drive they had to be conditioned.

Music was blaring from various honky-tonks. Ladies in sweeping skirts and modest bonnets, with market-baskets on their arms, tripped prettily along the wooden walks, seeking to avoid piles of dirt carelessly thrown out and dropping their eyes when some woman different from their class passed.

"It's exciting, isn't it, David?" Alice exclaimed, as she waited for the Rio Kid to reach them.

Bob Pryor, trailed by Celestino Mireles, came to them and grinned at Garrett and the girl.

"Howdy, folks!" he greeted. "I see yuh made it all right."

"Yeah," Garrett said slowly. "It ain't a bad run."

"Bob!" Alice suddenly exclaimed. "Why, you're hurt!"

The settlers left their wagons and came crowding around the Rio Kid. "Nothin' but a scratch," the Rio Kid assured them all, smiling.

"How'd it happen?" Alice asked.

"Oh, just a brush last night with a gunman who had a little too much red-eye," he replied carelessly.

Garrett envied the Rio Kid his reckless nature, his cool bravery. As for Alice, her eyes were big with excitement, and she was anxious about Pryor's injury.

46

A couple of riders passed close by on the road, headed out of Dodge.

"Who's that over there on the dun?" they all heard one of them ask.

"That's the Rio Kid, the feller who downed Keely and them others last night," the other rider replied. "Best shot on the Frontier, they say."

The story of the gunfights had spread the Rio Kid's name with rapidity throughout the wild town. Admiring eyes fixed upon him constantly, and he was becoming used to being pointed out to those who had missed the fracas. He was classed with Bat Masterson and Wyatt Earp. Fame had come to him in Dodge.

The new arrivals had a great deal of business to attend to—the registry of land titles, the arranging of credit, for they needed lumber and tools with which to build new homes. Norton Lane, Garrett, the Rio Kid and others of the settlers went about this, while the women began hunting for bargains in the way of food and clothing.

With the secret help of Dog Kelley, Earp and Masterson, the Rio Kid had arranged for credit with various firms. Though unknown to the settlers, Rio Kid had already taken up a collection and made down payments. Lane and his friends, however, with the fierce pride of pioneers believed they were being given full trust on their notes and on their crops, not yet in the ground. Actually it was because of the influential Kelley's guarantee that they were given everything they needed, with little cash necessary. Kelley and other Dodge City citizens, as well as the Rio Kid were gambling on the ability of these people to make a go of it and repay them later.

That night the settlers slept in their wagons. Early the following morning, with their wagons laden down with goods and more ordered, which would be picked up on other trips, Norton Lane and his friends started back for their new home site.

The Rio Kid rode along with them. He wanted to see them settled and to make sure all was well with them.

The sun came up on a crisp, fine day, and a thin sheet of ice gleamed on the little pools of the streams that ran

47

to the Arkansas River. When the cavalcade started, Dodge City was asleep, save for a few early risers. The distant bellowing of Texas cattle sounded from the camps outside the town.

They had not gone far when a horseman came riding toward them. The Rio Kid, out ahead with Celestino Mireles, recognized Frenchy Dupuy, the little gambler he had met in Dodge. Dupuy waved, and came trotting his horse toward them.

"Good morning!" he sang out. "How are you, Rio Kid?"

His smile was infectious and he was hearty and good-humored.

"Howdy, Frenchy," Pryor replied. "Where yuh bound so early?"

"I was over at Fort Dodge and the bugle routs you out at an ungodly hour," Dupuy said, smiling broadly. He nodded toward the wagons, lumbering along. "Those folks with you?"

"Yeah. Friends of mine from Dakota. Come to settle in Kansas."

"I see. Guess I'll ride a ways with you, Rio Kid, so we can talk."

"Glad to have yuh."

Garrett's wagon slowed as it reached the Rio Kid. Pryor introduced Dupuy to Alice Lane and to David. Frenchy was gallant and respectful. He took the girl's slim hand and touched his lips to it in Continental fashion, and she was astounded and pleased. The Rio Kid laughed to himself. Women liked such little attentions, he knew, and Alice would be no exception to the rule.

Dupuy soon met Norton Lane and some of the other settlers, and seemed much impressed. As he rode out ahead with Mireles and the Rio Kid, he learned something of their story, of the hard times they had encountered, and of the new lease of life offered when Pryor had led them to Kansas.

"Ah, I can see you are a great man!" Dupuy cried. "Yes, Rio Kid, you have a splendid heart. I wish I could help these people, too—yes, I mean it. Will you allow me?"

Pryor shrugged, amused inwardly at the little man's emotion. "Why, help yoreself, Frenchy. Everything counts. But yuh got to be careful how yuh offer 'em assistance. They're proud folks."

Frenchy Dupuy nodded, tears in his eyes.

"I understand them and admire them for it. I'll go along with you, if it's all the same to you, and see how they are fixed. I have some influence in Dodge, and maybe I can help."

So it was that the two-faced, evil Dupuy managed to ingratiate himself with the Rio Kid. And there was no outward indication that he was far more dangerous than an out-and-out enemy whose guns were in view.

# CHAPTER VII

## *A Fresh Start*

☐ The Rio Kid and Norton Lane had chosen a pretty site for the new settlement. The people had voted to call it Lanetown, for there was sentiment still attached to their late Dakota home, though their attempts to make a living there had been a failure.

The new home site in Kansas lay along the west bank of a wide, fresh creek that ran southward to the Arkansas, the dividing line between farmer districts and the land of steers. The hundreds of thousands of cattle that were coming up the Jones and Plummer Trail or were expected to come would never do any good to crops. Always there had been friction on the various trails, too, when herds got out of hand and broke into the fields, destroying crops. The now legally established divide would prevent clashes.

There was a belt of timber along the stream that would prove valuable. And buffalo chips, to be used as fuel could be picked up from the plains. Back from the creek valley rose some low hills which would furnish protection for stock during the winter.

Tents and rough shelters had been thrown up, and some of the group had been left there to watch the camp. As the returning travelers splashed across the ford at the creek children ran out into the stream to meet the triumphant wagoneers. Older people stood on the bank and cheered as Norton Lane and his drivers waved their hats, showing by gestures how successful they had been. The incoming supplies meant life or death for them, a new lease on existence, a fresh start.

It was nearly sundown when the wagoneers reached the settlement. Every hand was needed, and all set to work. Even after a quick supper they kept on laboring by the light of big fires.

After a few hours' sleep, they rose in the first streaks of the new day and resumed. There was endless toil in such a place. Ground had to be broken, buildings started, stones rolled, the stock cared for, food prepared and carefully stored. There were a million tasks.

The Rio Kid and Mireles lent their aid wherever they were needed, which was everywhere. Shelter for both humans and animals must go up; and fuel had to be collected or marked for future cutting. There were some stands of cottonwoods and scrub oaks in the hills, and in the afternoon the Rio Kid, accompanied by Frenchy Dupuy, rode up to check on them.

Dupuy had turned to and worked with a will, assisting the settlers. All liked him. They liked his quick smile and the jest always on his lips. His hands were skillful, too.

After a short look through the hills, which ran back for some miles, and which had been filed on by some of the new settlers when they went to Dodge, the Rio Kid returned to camp. It seemed a welter of confusion. Piles of lumber and bags of supplies lay about, walked over by children and workers and by investigating dogs and other animals. But order was arising from it all, as individual settlers took what they needed and went to their various sites to start their homes.

Next morning, Dupuy offered to help with the stock, for the animals were to be driven into the hills where the herbage was better. Also, the hills would form a natural corral so the beasts would not stray too far while their owners were busy.

Dupuy left that morning and was gone all day. He returned, exhausted and dirt-stained, at dark.

"When do you expect to go back to Dodge?" he asked the Rio Kid. "I've got an appointment there tomorrow night that I can't miss."

"Oh, I'll be along in a couple days, I reckon. The election's due soon and I don't want to miss it. From what Kelley and the others say it'll be real sport. See yuh then."

"All right. When I'm free I expect to visit the folks here and help some more. They're fine people."

The Rio Kid nodded. Such people deserved a chance. That was all they needed to win.

Frenchy Dupuy left at sunrise. Three days later the Rio Kid, having seen his friends well started in their new home, saddled up Saber and headed for Dodge. His faithful companion, Mireles, was at his dun's heels.

He found Dodge in greater turmoil than usual, terrifically excited over the coming election. Street orators were bawling in the plaza, and fights were of common occurrence between partisans.

James Dog Kelley had a strong following. His opponent, however, a huge, walrus-mustached fellow with dull blue eyes, was making the most extravagant promises as to what he would accomplish if made mayor. The South Side, the shady element, and the Texas drovers who liked a wide-open town were against Kelley's moderation faction.

Rumor had it that behind Kelley's rival was a recent arrival in Dodge, a man named Phillip Harrison. Harrison's name was being whispered about town as the real politico against Kelley. The candidate was but a front, a local character the voters knew.

"I'd like to get a peek at this Harrison hombre," remarked the Rio Kid.

He was sitting in Dog Kelley's with Frenchy Dupuy, Bat Masterson and a couple of other friends. He was enjoying the excitement hugely, and had enlisted in Dog Kelley's ranks, ready to take his part in the trouble that seemed bound to come. For it was known that the other side would use every possible means to win, fair or foul. Strong-arm men to protect the voters from intimidation —and worse—would be needed, and the Rio Kid was one of them, a deputy marshal for the week of the election.

"That's easy," said Kelley. "There's Harrison now."

"Yeah, that's him," corroborated Dupuy. "The tall one."

The Rio Kid stared at Harrison. The fellow was clad in a black broadcloth suit and a black felt hat with a wide brim. He wore a white ruffled shirt and stock, and fine calfskin boots. His body was long, with wide, bony shoulders slightly stooped. He was clean-shaven and his hair, what showed under the black Stetson, was brown, with light streaks running through it.

"He looks like a smart customer," remarked Pryor. "Dog, yuh'll have to go some to beat him to the finish line, I'm thinkin'. Let's have a drink on it."

The Rio Kid, even facing the man he wanted so grimly to meet, could have no inkling that Harrison was Valentine Everts, the crooked contractor he was after. The changed appearance, the bleached hair, the absence of spectacles and different clothing made a different man of Everts than the man who had been described to the Rio Kid.

After another drink, Pryor rose and went out on patrol. He was proud of the deputy's badge glinting on his vest, proud of his chance to help keep order in Dodge. He meant to see to it that the Texas cowboys and other wild ones did not hurrah the town and kill any innocent bystanders.

It was close to dawn when he turned in, sleeping in the rear room of Dog Kelley's place. He woke around noon, washed up and went out to hunt some breakfast. A man called to him from across the way. Turning, the Rio Kid saw Norton Lane. The farmer's face showed that he was worried.

"Oh, Rio Kid!" cried Lane, hurrying to meet him. "I'm all-fired glad to see you!"

"What's up, Lane?"

53

"It's Alice—I'm mighty upset about her. She's here, in Dodge. She insisted on comin' to town, says she means to be a singer. I don't know what to do."

"Well, doggone my hide!"

The Rio Kid was startled. "It's sort of my fault," he thought, but aloud he said, "Well, Lane, she has a mighty fine voice. I've heard her singin' a lot and never heard a prettier voice."

"Yes, but it ain't respectable! She's too young to stay here in Dodge alone, and her mother and me can't give up the new farm we got."

"Where is she now?"

"Over at the drygoods store, buyin' a new dress."

"Would yuh let her stay if we were able to make it right for her? Yuh don't want to stampede her, Lane. Yuh can't do it with young folks when they get their mind set on a thing. She might run off somewheres on her own, and that wouldn't do at all."

Norton Lane nodded. "I savvy that. It's got me in a dither."

"Wait here for me then, till I talk to a friend of mine."

The Rio Kid found Dog Kelley busy in his office, going over the receipts of the night before. Kelley greeted the Kid with gusto, and shoved a bottle and cigar box toward him. But the Rio Kid shook his head.

"I got a favor to ask, Dog," he said.

"Anything at all, Rio Kid."

"There's a young lady here, a daughter of a friend of mine, Norton Lane—told yuh of him, the head of that bunch of farmers from Dakota, that yuh chipped in to help. She's got her mind set on bein' a singer and I wondered if yuh could let her do a piece in the Alhambra here?"

Kelley whistled. "Is she any good?"

"Swell. We could sort of keep an eye on her. And I thought she might board at yore place so's yore wife could watch over her. If she sings early, why, the boys won't be so all-fired crazy as later on."

Dog Kelley nodded. "All right, Rio Kid. I'll do it."

Alice was outside with her father when Pryor

emerged. She came forward to greet him, smiling up into his handsome eyes.

"It's all fixed," the Rio Kid said. "Come in and meet Dog Kelley, yore new boss, Alice."

She was delighted, and even Norton Lane was satisfied with the arrangement. He was in a hurry to return to his new farm, for there were uncounted things to be done.

That evening the Rio Kid sat with Bat Masterson and his friends, listening to Alice Lane sing. The girl's beauty and freshness, her fine voice, thrilled the spectators. It was still early and the men were sober enough to appreciate her. The Rio Kid congratulated her and saw her safely home to Mrs. Kelley. Then he went out on street patrol, for the fever in Dodge was rising to explosive point.

Pausing to turn at the southeast corner of the plaza, jostling crowds of excited men in the streets and on the sidewalks with their wooden awning extensions, the Rio Kid heard a series of gunshots and high-pitched screams above the din of the roaring cow country metropolis. He ran for the spot, just in time to see Ed Masterson, Bat's younger brother, staggering against a rail.

Drawing a Colt, the Rio Kid raced toward his friend and fellow deputy marshal. But Ed thumbed his Colt hammer and a crimson-faced cowboy who had been drinking heavily took the lead in the middle. He folded up, dead.

But even as his opponent fell, Ed Masterson crumpled up on the sidewalk, arms extended.

The shouting crowd paused for a moment, silenced by sudden death, but only those in the immediate vicinity who had seen the affray with their own eyes were affected. Shootings were far too common in Dodge to hold interest for long.

The Rio Kid bent over Ed Masterson, who was mortally wounded. Ed's brother Bat, sheriff for Ford County, rushed across to the spot, and knelt, but his brother could no longer speak.

They carried the dying marshal inside Kelley's place, but he did not long survive.

"Tough, Bat," murmured the Rio Kid.

Bat Masterson held himself in steel control. His pale-blue eyes were like cold agates.

"I knew it," he said to Pryor. "Ed wasn't the type for this kinda work, Rio Kid. He stopped to argue with that blasted fool from the Rio Grande."

The Rio Kid nodded. He understood that such work required an icy brain with quick instantaneous reactions.

A man who hesitated to kill, because of pity or because of no desire to slay a fellow creature before giving him time to draw and fire his gun, was doomed. A marshal of Dodge must know whom and when to shoot. That took an instinct, then experience.

Both Bat Masterson and the Rio Kid possessed these. But Ed Masterson had not.

The youngster had tried to talk the liquor-maddened cowboy into reasonableness and so had died.

# CHAPTER VIII

## Attack

☐ Election day dawned cold and clear. Buffalo robes were a necessity in the icy wind that swept the frozen prairie. Men went warmly clad, or hugged the red-hot stoves in their homes.

Girded and ready for action, Bob Pryor, the Rio Kid, started his patrol to watch the polls. It was not long before trouble started. A big gang of cowboys, whose legal residence was not within a thousand miles of Kansas tore in from the South Side and took over a polling place, insisting they had the right to vote for the mayor of Dodge.

City marshals drew in, walking like so many panthers, guns glinting in readiness. Proof of residence had to be produced, which was something the cowboys could not give.

In the resulting fracas, one man was wounded by gunshot, and Neal Brown got a knife cut on his arm.

Dutch Henry's gang was in town, as well. Each moment the police grew busier and busier. Around noon Bat Masterson called a conference during a slight lull when the disturbers paused for refreshments.

"I'm plumb wore out," growled Bat, mopping the dew from his brow, for in spite of the cold outside, the constant physical exertion kept him and his men warmed up. "Chasin' off repeaters and crooks who ain't got the shadow of a right to vote in Dodge. We've had two men wounded already, and they're whittlin' us down. There ain't so many of us as there are of them and the polls don't shut till six o'clock. Anybody got any ideas?"

The Rio Kid grinned and raised a hand.

"I have, Bat. It might help some."

"What is it?"

"Let me go over to the South Side and arrest Phil Harrison. It's known he's behind Kelley's opponent and most of the trouble-makers come from there. It'd throw 'em into confusion, mebbe, to have their brains lopped off."

Bat turned this over in his alert mind. Earp nodded, seeing the logic in such police strategy.

"The Rio Kid always goes straight to the heart of a fuss," he murmured.

"There's no judge sittin' today, 'count it's election," continued Pryor, "so's he couldn't pay his fine and walk out on us. By tomorrow the votin' will be over with and we'll turn him loose."

"Well, it might work," agreed Masterson, a little reluctantly. "But we can't let yuh try it alone. We'll tag along. Let's ride. It ain't far."

They hurriedly got horses and started for the South Side, which hummed with excitement. Painted women hung from the windows, cheering at the passing men. The dives teemed with the roughs who frequented the district.

Straight toward his objective traveled the Rio Kid. He had, by inquiry, ascertained where Harrison's headquarters were in the back room of a saloon.

Swiftly the officers, a dozen of them and every one a known crack shot, made for the place. The Rio Kid turned into the side alley and came up at the back. A group of men were hanging around the door, but made way in surprise as the determined officers drove in.

"There's Dutch Henry, Bat—grab him!" cried the Rio Kid.

He jumped into a square room. At a table sat Harrison, hat off, smoking a black stogie. Some tough-looking

58

fellows were listening to orders but looked up, as did Harrison, at the lithe Rio Kid's entrance.

"Aw right, Dutch—yuh're comin' to the calaboose," Bat Masterson's sharp voice declared out in the hall.

There was no shot. Evidently the horse thief did not dare to shoot it out with Bat.

The Rio Kid stood, feet spread, and hands hanging easily at his thighs, close to the Army Colts in their supple holsters there. Harrison met his straight glance, held it a moment, then turned red.

"Well—what is it?" he growled, harshly.

"Yuh're under arrest, Harrison," the Rio Kid said coldly, "for disorderly conduct and incitin' riots!"

Dangerous as the situation was, the Rio Kid found it rich with humor. Politics was hardly a clean game, locally or otherwise, at the time. Harrison, who was inciting reckless cowboys and ringers to vote, paying them, was liable to such arrest, but it also was a smart campaign trick.

When he ordered Harrison to surrender, the Rio Kid knew that at the drop of a hat the gunmen around might start shooting. But he was ready.

"What!" snarled Harrison, unable to believe his ears.

His cronies froze. Close behind the Rio Kid they saw Neal Brown, Wyatt Earp, Doc Holliday, Bat Masterson and other officers of Dodge. Anyone who started trouble would have to be prepared to finish it. Dutch Henry had given in, and waited, disarmed, in the hall.

"Yuh're goin' to spend the rest of the day in the calaboose, instead of sendin' Texas men to gun us," snapped the Rio Kid.

In the next tense moments Phil Harrison glared in fury at the Rio Kid, measuring him, seeking a loophole.

Suddenly Harrison dropped his eyes, and pushed back his chair.

"All right," he said. "I'll go."

The Rio Kid had backed him into a hole and made him pull his head in, according to the parlance of Dodge.

Between the stalking officers walked the two important prisoners, Dutch Henry and Phil Harrison, ringleaders of the criminal faction which opposed Dog Kelley. They were whisked across the Santa Fe tracks and placed behind bars, with locked doors and a guard.

Fury, insane rage, seized upon the South Side as news of the arrests spread like wildfire. A dozen mobs gathered, harangued by loud-voiced men, but no one took any action. Their anger was expressed by hot words rather than gunsmoke.

Through the afternoon the Rio Kid and his friends had some trouble but they were able to handle it easily enough. And when the polls closed just after dark fell over the town, they knew they had won.

When the votes were counted, Dog Kelley had been elected Mayor of Dodge City, and the better element had triumphed.

Then riotous celebration burst in full bloom over the Babylon of the Plains.

It lasted all night. By dawn the plaza and streets were filled with rubble, smashed whiskey and beer bottles, hats, papers, discarded clothing. Bonfires had raged to the sky, threatening the rickety frame buildings, but had been quenched.

Worn out, jaded by the terrific excitement, Dodge City citizens flung themselves down to sleep wherever they happened to be. . . .

The evening following James Kelley's election as Mayor of Dodge City, a victory for the more conservative and decent folk of the settlement, was comparatively quiet.

Phil Harrison, or Valentine Everts, in a black mood, for fury was burning his evil soul, sat with his crony and spy, Frenchy Dupuy, in a secret place on the South Side. At midnight they were drinking. Everts was ranting against the Rio Kid, coming back again and again to that sore point.

"I'll go out and kill him myself!" he snarled.

Dupuy watched him, his eyes narrowed.

"He's tough, Boss. A hard man to come up on. Besides, Dog Kelley's given orders to Earp and the other marshals to keep an eye peeled when the Rio Kid's on patrol.

They're suspicious on account of those two tries we made for him. But he never sleeps in the same place twice, since we nearly got him. Now the election's over, though, I don't reckon Pryor'll stay on the police force."

"I'll never rest easy till he's dead!" growled Everts.

Dupuy shrugged. "That may be so. He doesn't savvy yet that you're the man who ran the Sunrise Arms. If he did, you wouldn't be sittin' here now."

Everts scowled at his aide. "Blast him! That election was mighty close. I had plenty more tricks up my sleeve and we might have swung it our way if the Rio Kid hadn't pulled that arrest. Dutch and I spent the whole afternoon and night in that filthy jail. There goes a cool million out of my hands, thanks to him. The vice in Dodge is worth anything you want to mention."

Dupuy leaned forward across the table, speaking earnestly.

"Why don't you try what I suggested, Boss? I tell you, there's more than a million in it."

"It means a lot of dangerous work."

"It's a cinch, though. You got Dutch Henry and his gang lined up, and Dutch needs something to do. Now we're sunk in Dodge, Dutch'll snap it up. It'll hurt the Rio Kid worse than bullets, for he has his heart set on puttin' those farmers on their feet and givin' 'em a fresh start. It would be a real defeat to him and hurt his pride. I tell you, I know it. Wasn't I out there with him? He acts like a hen with a bunch of chicks to take care of."

"Huh!"

Everts took a long swig from the bottle, and his brow was wrinkled with thought. Suddenly he slammed his fist on the table.

"You're right. I'm sittin' here like a fool when I ought to be in action. Tell Dutch I want to talk to him. . . ."

An hour later, Val Everts, clad in a dark cape and with his hat strapped low against the wind, rode out of Dodge in the darkness. A cold wind swept the flats along the Arkansas. About him were red glows, marking blanket camps of Texas drovers.

Dutch Henry was at the rendezvous five miles west of

61

Dodge. He had brought a number of his men with him, and more were coming. While they waited for the gunmen, Everts and Dutch elaborated on their plans.

"We'll feel 'em out tomorrow night," said Everts. "In the meantime, Dupuy'll check further."

"It may draw the Rio Kid out of Dodge," observed Henry, a cigarette glowing red in his hard lips.

"So much the better. In fact, we'll be all ready for him, curse his hide."

They started west, sixty dark-clad, muffled riders crossing the plains.

At break of the new day, they made for some stretches of timber along the north bank of the Arkansas River and went into camp to sleep and eat.

After dark they were again on their way, and arrived on the low slope overlooking Norton Lane's new settlement and the creek when the place was silver in the moonlight. The rough little shacks and tents were dark, for the farmers turned in early after their day of hard toil.

"That the place?" growled Everts.

"Yeah, this is it," replied Henry. "Frenchy told me just how to hit it."

They could look down over the creek and see the domes of the hills to the west, blackly rising against the sky.

"All right, boys," Dutch Henry said, turning to his men, who had bunched up behind him. "Split up into pairs and circulate down there and back through the hills. Keep it quiet. Pick up as many hosses as yuh see and run 'em south toward the Territory. We'll meet at the reg'lar place north of the Cimarron. Shoot down anybody who shows his head, savvy?"

The killers pulled up their bandannas as masks. Fierce eyes glinted as pistols were cocked, ready for action. They started their horses across the creek ford, and spread out through the area, hunting for stock to run off.

Everts stayed close to Dutch Henry, the chief of the horse thieves. Several especially tough gunmen rode as Dutch's bodyguard, and they pushed to the right, toward a farmer's new shack.

Dutch went to the barn behind the place, and the door was opened. There were five horses inside, and they were brought out, their muzzles bound with cloth. However, the stamping of the hoofs awakened the owner.

"Watch it!" warned Dutch, turning.

A door squeaked and the leather hinges on which it swung rasped the warning.

"Hey, you! What in tarnation you doin' out there?"

A settler, shotgun in hand, stood in the opening, and quickly diagnosed the situation.

"Horse thieves!" he bawled, throwing his shotgun to his shoulder.

Everts fired from the hip. The shotgun roared, but the flash was low and the scattering buckshot missed the target. Three Colts banged on the echo, but the man in the door was already falling, killed by Everts' bullet.

A woman began to scream and shouts came from neighboring houses.

"Take them hosses straight through, Buck," ordered Dutch. "We'll amuse 'em."

Spurring through the settlement, guns blaring, the bandits shot at living targets, men who ran out to fight them off. As the opposition grew, the horse thieves retreated, but not until they had left confusion and death in their wake.

Everts glanced back at the aroused place.

"That'll do for a start," he growled.

# CHAPTER IX

## *Alarm*

☐ Resting up after the strenuous election in which he had contributed toward Dog Kelley's victory in Dodge, the Rio Kid began wondering about his charges at Lanetown, the new development west of the city.

Alice was as happy as a lark, singing in Kelley's place each evening. Mrs. Kelley watched over her, cared for her. She was under the protection of the Rio Kid, Bat Masterson and Wyatt Earp, and no man dared so much as lift an eyebrow at the girl.

Pryor had expected that Phil Harrison and Dutch Henry might try to retaliate for his coup on election day, but the grapevine had it that they had left Dodge.

It was evening, and the Rio Kid sat at his usual table, held for him by Dog Kelley, listening to Alice Lane as she sang. She wore a long blue dress and her cheeks sparkled with color and happiness. Now and then she would glance toward him and he would smile back at her in approval.

The men in the place were listening quietly. They had deep respect for a decent woman.

"Hullo, Rio Kid," a low voice said, suddenly, and Bob Pryor looked around sharply. He grinned as he recognized Dave Garrett.

"Dave! Mighty glad to see yuh! Siddown and wet yore whistle. Alice looks pretty as a picture, don't she?"

Garrett's blue eyes, once so eager, were shadowed, opaque. He seemed to be under constraint with the Rio Kid, who quickly sensed that Garrett was uneasy.

The young man was different from his usual self and the Rio Kid realized that it was because Dave had changed not only his manner but his clothing. He wore a leather cowboy jacket, a Stetson, half-boots with spurs, and black pants tucked into the flaps. About his waist was strapped a cartridge belt, with a brand-new Colt .45 revolver, Frontier model, reposing in the stiff brown holster.

For a minute the Rio Kid was amused.

"You—" he began, then noted the somber glow in Garrett's eyes as he watched Alice Lane.

Pryor had meant to tease him, tell him he looked like a marshal. But he liked Dave and did not wish to hurt his feelings and Garrett was plainly in deadly earnest.

"Siddown," he invited again.

Garrett shook his head.

"I come to town with an important message. Lane sent me. Is Bat Masterson, the sheriff, around? I went to the City Hall and they said to tell him my message. It's a county affair."

"What's wrong?"

"Last night a passel of horse thieves attacked us and killed Charlie Gregory and wounded Ike Vernon. They run off about eighteen head of stock. Some of the boys set out after 'em but we can't spare many hands and Lane figgered we needed help."

"Huh?" The Rio Kid got up, instantly worried about his settler friends. "I know where to find Bat. He's playin' monte in the Annex. C'mon."

Bat Masterson received the news with a frown.

"So that's where Dutch went to," he growled. "I'll swear in a posse in the mornin' and go after 'em, Garrett."

"Count me in, Bat, and Mireles, too," said the Rio Kid.

"All right. We'll be startin' at dawn."

"What's up, gents?"

65

Dog Kelley came over, and listened to the tale which Dave Garrett had brought in.

"Yuh know Dave Garrett?" asked Pryor. "He's a first-class friend of mine, Dog."

"The place is yores, feller." The mayor smiled, shaking hands heartily with the young man. "Come have a drink on the house."

"Thanks, Mr. Kelley. I will."

Garrett left the Rio Kid, who stared after him with a troubled face.

"He's actin' plumb queer," he mused. "And I reckon it's on account of Alice. Jealous, no doubt of it, and blames me for her bein' here."

Turning it over, the Rio Kid found that he was pretty fond of the girl himself. He had seen her a good deal during the days she had been in Dodge and, come to think of it, she rather seemed to admire him. At least she always had a smile ready for him.

"She's a beauty," he thought.

Then he shook his head. Marriage meant giving up the wild ways of the Frontier. He could no longer play the devil, and gunfight, flitting from spot to spot, if he married and settled down.

The Rio Kid turned in early that night. He was not on patrol as a deputy in Dodge for, with the election over, the regular police force was adequate. He wanted to be fresh for the chase after the horse thieves, a chase which might run into a week or ten days. . . .

Sheriff Masterson, who alternated his duties as police chief with volunteer work on the Dodge City police force, was in his office right after breakfast the next day, swearing in deputies for the pursuit after the killers and bandits who had attacked Lanetown.

The Rio Kid and Celestino Mireles were among the first to take the oath and be handed badges. They had their guns and horses ready, and during the time Bat was busy filling out his force of fighting men, the Rio Kid ate breakfast, then went to hunt for Dave Garrett, whom he had not seen since the previous evening.

He found Garrett hanging around Dog Kelley's. The place was deserted save for a sweeper.

"Mornin', Dave," he greeted. "We're ridin' out in the next hour. Why don't yuh come along? We'll drop yuh off at home."

Garrett shook his head. "I reckon I'm not goin' back there," he said coolly.

"What yuh mean?"

"I'm goin' to stay in Dodge. Thanks for interducin' me to Mayor Kelley. He's a fine feller."

The Rio Kid shrugged. He saw how it stood. Dave thought more of Alice than he did of making a success of farming, and was determined to be near the girl. Pryor did not blame him.

"All right, Dave," he said mildly. "Anything I can do, let me know."

He did not try to prevail on Garrett to go with the posse in pursuit of the bandits, for Masterson would want only experienced fighters, and Garrett was green.

Half an hour later twenty men, led by Bat Masterson and the Rio Kid, rode out of Dodge City, westward toward Lanetown.

Norton Lane had sent word that fifty robbers had attacked, and Masterson figured that his gun veterans could handle that number, even if they came up with them all at once. It was unlikely that this would happen, since horse thieves usually scattered after a raid.

Dutch Henry was known to be particularly clever at evading pursuit and justice. He had arrangements with gangs of horse thieves in Texas and they would meet, one band riding north, the other south, swap stolen stock, and return to their own haunts, with all proof gone.

The Rio Kid and Bat Masterson made a swift trip of it, pulling into Lanetown before dark. Norton Lane met them, shook hands. The posse dismounted to rest their horses and stretch after the hard run.

The people had been sadly shocked by the night attack. The death of a respected member of the community had upset them all. Besides, they had lost animals which they sorely needed.

67

The Rio Kid introduced his friends to the distinguished frontiersmen and scouts who made up Masterson's party. Such men as Jim Hanrahan, "Old Man" Keeler, Virgil Earp, one of Wyatt's brothers—Wyatt himself had been held in town on important law work—made up the party. Many were buffalo hunters in season, every one was a crack shot with revolver and rifle. All of them knew of the Lane settlers, too, who had been sponsored by the Rio Kid and leading Dodge City citizens.

After resting for the night, Bat Masterson called his fighters together. They had breakfast, saddled up and, heavily armed, took the cold trail of the bandits. A small party of men from Lanetown had trailed the thieves for fifteen miles, across the Arkansas, but had lost the sign in the rough, hilly country to the south.

With provisions such as hard tack and jerked beef in their saddle-bags, the expert marksmen could live off wild game, for weeks if necessary, as there was plenty of water in the streams.

It was open riding through the first day. They swam the icy Arkansas River and pressed on, with scouts out in approved military style.

Late in the afternoon of their second day out from Lanetown, the Rio Kid was in advance of the main party under Bat Masterson. His keen blue eyes, trained to scout work, were on the faint markings left by the party of thieves which had struck the farming community of his friends.

The telltale indentations, crusted by the wind and frost of several days, could hardly have been noticed by an inexpert eye. Long spaces had to be skipped, but each time the Rio Kid picked up the sign again.

Before him loomed some long, ridgelike hills, with gray rocks showing in the reddish-gray earth, and scrub timber, with dead leaves rattling in the breeze, on their shanks. It was splendid riding weather, cold and crisp. The ground was frozen at the moment, in this season of alternate thaw and freeze.

The Rio Kid glanced up at the deserted, uninviting hills. They seemed utterly devoid of life. He looked down again at the sign. It was at least four days old; probably five.

The trail of the horse thieves swung to his right as he faced south, and entered the parallel ridges, disappearing from vision around the constricted northern opening. By swinging a quarter of a mile to the left, it would have been possible to head in the same direction and avoid the worst of the rough going. The horse thieves were no doubt headed for Indian Territory, the paradise of such fellows.

"Reckon they wanted to keep out of sight as much as they could," decided Pryor, and started Saber on to the cut.

Behind him, the scouts followed, trusting to his keenness.

The wind was from the west, blowing on his right cheek as he headed through. As he came to the blufflike flanks of the hills, one at either side looming over him, he looked up. They were silent and bare. He passed through and saw before him a narrow, rocky way that wound up and reached a saddle of ground which afforded a passage. The trail was in here, the sign quite readable.

"Let's go, Saber," he muttered. "We have to move. Them fellers are way ahead, but—"

Suddenly the dun wrinkled the black stripe which ran the length of his back. The Rio Kid's eyes narrowed and he instantly grew alert, a hand dropping to his gun butt as he searched every inch of the surrounding slopes. He knew that danger signal which Saber had flashed him. The animal senses of the horse had caught something which no human could detect.

Bat Masterson, who was riding leisurely at the front of his company, and who had drawn up some when the Rio Kid had halted outside the cut, caught up with the Kid when he paused.

"What's up?" Masterson asked. "Yuh dreamin'?"

"Nope, Bat. But the dun says it ain't safe."

Masterson, on his favorite buckskin, Houston, looked quickly about. Then he got from saddle to investigate the sign by dropping to his hands and knees and studying it closely. The Rio Kid followed suit, trailing his reins on the ground.

Bat shook his head as he straightened up.

"This trail's as cold as a mother-in-law's heart," he declared. "There ain't nothin'—"

"Look out!" shouted Virgil Earp, from the rear of the column.

Guns suddenly roared, filling the ravine with raging fury. And as suddenly the ridge tops swarmed with enemies, masked men whose carbines pointed down at the posse.

# CHAPTER X

## *Retreat*

☐ On foot, and some yards from his horse, the Rio Kid ripped out his pistol and began hastily shooting up at the targets he could see, the Stetsons and masked faces of riflemen lining the ridges.

"Ride for it, boys!" he bellowed over the din of the battle. "It's an ambush!"

Two men had fallen from their saddles at the first volley, and lay silent, on the rocky way. One had a smashed brain-pan, another had received lead through the heart. Several others of the posse had felt the sting of enemy bullets but kept their seats, iron knees gripping the leather.

Three horses had been hit, dismounting their riders. One seized the bridle of a dead man's animal and vaulted to the saddle, while the other two leaped up behind friends for the escape.

The Rio Kid and Bat Masterson had been farthest into the ambush cut and both had been dismounted. Masterson, his Colt coolly snarling replies to the foe, and making a hit with every explosion, reached his horse, Houston, and mounted. He moved with speed, but was not panicky. He wasted no instant by the shakiness brought by fear.

The Rio Kid, straightening up to run, found that his

gun-belt had slipped down low around his thighs, impeding him. He had loosened it for comfort while riding.

He had to pause, pull it up and tighten the buckle. A slug cut a hole in his hat, while another that had been aimed at his heart burned along his upper left arm.

"Come on!" called Bat Masterson, slowing to help his friend. "We'll have tea somewheres else!"

The other possemen were retreating, dashing back for the exit. Pistols, rifles and buffalo guns made a roaring din. The Rio Kid, ringed about with lead, leaped on the back of the snorting, excited dun and spurted after Houston.

They shot back at the enemy as they ran. Alongside the rocky trail lay another victim of the ambush. And Celestino Mireles, who had waited for the Rio Kid, was suddenly set afoot as his horse shrieked and crashed to the earth.

The Rio Kid pulled up Saber, and the Mexican youth sprang up behind Pryor. Then they spurted through the bluff gates and were able to ride for safety, followed by the bullets and jeering cries of the bandits.

It was a sadly battered party that collected, out of easy gunshot, on the plain above the ambush hills. Three of their number had been killed, and seven others had more or less serious wounds. Four horses were gone, while others had been hurt.

Icy rage burned in the Rio Kid's heart. So great was his fury that he did not feel the wounds where hostile bullets had slashed him. He cursed the horse thieves as he shoved fresh shells into his hot Colts.

"Bat," he growled, "that was my fault. I was in the lead."

"Don't talk like a fool," Masterson said sharply. "No more yore fault than mine, Rio Kid. It was a clever trap, best I ever seen. Why, I'da got up on the stand and took my oath that trail was four days old! If yore dun hadn't give that warnin', we'd all be dead right now. We wasn't quite far enough in but they had to shoot, I reckon, seein' we were suspicious."

"They musta laid it like that for us to foller, that's all, Bat," said Pryor. "Then they met more of their friends comin' up the other direction and doubled around to the ridges. Yuh savvy any of 'em?"

"I was sort of absent-minded about makin' a study of 'em in there," drawled Bat, "but I think I reckernized Tom Owens. He's Dutch Henry's closest pard. I don't doubt it's the main Owens-Henry band."

"There're at least three hundred of 'em back there," Virgil Earp growled.

"And here they come!" shouted Jim Hanrahan, who was nursing a bleeding hand.

Wild riders appeared, sweeping around the bulge of the hills. Their masks were up and they opened a long-range carbine fire as they moved on the smashed posse.

"Come on, boys!" Bat Masterson ordered. "We'll show 'em what a runnin' fight is if that's what they want."

They began their retreat north, back toward Lanetown and Dodge City. To fight such a number of desperate killers was impossible. All chance of surprise was gone. The shoe had been on the other foot.

Out in the open, however, it was a different story from the fiasco in the constricted ravine. Any bandit who dared get within range of the scouts' guns received a token in the form of a bullet. The ravening rustler horde stayed behind the depleted posse as they rode slowly, sturdily, off across the plain.

"I don't see Dutch Henry and Tom Owens, but that's their combined gang," declared Bat Masterson.

He raised his carbine and laconically shot a bandit who had ventured too near for his own health, out of the saddle. The range was long and most men would have missed, but Bat Masterson was a genius with firearms.

"I reckon," Bat said to the Rio Kid, "the chiefs are lyin' back in the hills."

Several times the gunmen lieutenants sought to whip their killers into rushing the party of veterans but the toll the Rio Kid and his pards took was terrific, and each dash ended in fiasco for the larger bunch.

But for three hours, until dark closed in on the land, they kept up the pursuit. The sun sank and stars twinkled out, with a big yellow area on the horizon where the moon was coming up. The scouts speeded up their horses, veering off course. The Rio Kid stayed at the rear of the column, to watch there.

"They're givin' us up," he muttered, as he heard no sounds from the enemy after half an hour.

The battered band under the Rio Kid and Bat Masterson rode on across a cold, deserted land. Two of the men were badly wounded, suffering from the night frost and fatigue after the fight and the enforced ride. They could scarcely stay in leather, and Bat Masterson consulted in a low voice with Bob Pryor.

"What yuh reckon we better do? We can't camp here."

"Yuh mean to head straight for Dodge, Bat?"

"Yeah," growled Bat, his eyes as frosty as the sky. "I want to break even with Dutch and that gang of cheap gun-fighters."

"The nearest shelter now is Lanetown," suggested the Rio Kid. "I want to go there, anyway, to warn them folks what a big gang is operatin' around here. A surprise attack by such a bunch might wipe 'em out entirely. S'pose I take Mireles and the worst wounded and head for there? You keep on with the ones who want to ride for Dodge."

"All right. First we better pause, though, and warm up some coffee. The devil with anything else."

They built a small, quick fire in a buffalo wallow, screening the flame with blankets, and heated water, mixing up some sort of hot drink. It refreshed the weary riders, and in an hour they started on again, the Rio Kid with two almost mortally wounded strapped to their saddles and muffled in blankets. Masterson and the main crew said good-by and cut toward Dodge.

It was daylight before Mireles and the Rio Kid splashed across the creek into Lanetown. Their two charges were unconscious, hanging over their horses and fastened on with lariats.

Frenchy Dupuy came running out of Norton Lane's cabin to greet the Rio Kid.

"Hi, there, Rio Kid!" the little man cried. "Where you been? I was worried about you."

"Mornin', Frenchy."

Pryor's lips were blue with cold and his hands, despite the gauntlets he wore, were so stiff he could scarcely close his fingers on the reins. Norton Lane appeared from a nearby stable and hurried to his side.

"Pryor! What's wrong?"

"Take care of those boys and I'll tell yuh."

Other settlers gathered about. Willing hands lifted the injured down and carried them inside, to be warmed and nursed.

A hot drink braced the Rio Kid, though sleep tugged at his eyelids.

"How'd yuh happen to wander over here, Frenchy?" he inquired.

"Me? I was sittin' in a poker game at the Fort, and it took me all one day and a night to win the colonel's salary. When I got back to Dodge, you and Bat had been gone for hours. I heard of the trouble here and thought maybe I could help out. Tried to trail you and ended up at Lane's."

"Good. We can use every hand. There's three hundred of them hoss thieves around and when I'm rested some, I'll figger out what to do."

He fell asleep the instant his head touched the blanket laid near the warm stove. Mireles was already dead to the world.

There was no danger in the homely sounds about him, the soft tread of women going about their tasks, the shouts of herders and the stamp of hoofs. The Rio Kid slept all day and woke at dusk, refreshed and, save for a slight stiffness in his limbs from the hard ride, in the cold, entirely himself.

Mireles was squatted close by, drinking a large cup of steaming coffee. Bob Pryor went for the same dose, stoking up.

Frenchy Dupuy rode up and dismounted. He entered the shack while Pryor was rolling a smoke. The little man's cheeks were crimson from the icy air.

"Anything I can do," said Dupuy, "tell me."

"All right. First I want to talk to Lane. We've got to organize a defense for these folks, in case them devils come back some dark night."

"But—why should they bother to attack such poor people as these?" Dupuy demanded incredulously.

"I dunno. All I savvy is that fifty of Dutch Henry's gang run off a passel of hosses from here and shot a couple of farmers, which set the sheriff and me on their trail. They had as pretty an ambush as I ever saw set for us. Why should they have bothered with all that, when they coulda scattered and got away with the hosses? I figger they hit here to draw Masterson and me after 'em. No profit for three hundred gunnies in a couple dozen farm plugs."

"I see your point," agreed Frenchy. He bit his mustache nervously. "And yet—I don't believe they'll come back here."

Norton Lane came in, followed by a group of his friends. The Rio Kid had told the leader to gather his fighters together for instructions.

Military experience, obtained during the long years of the Civil War as a scout, and his earlier life on the Rio Grande stood the Rio Kid in good stead. He swiftly arranged an alarm system whereby the farmers would take turns at picket duty at night while the rest, upon hearing a signal—one shot followed by two quick reports—would rush to that point for defense.

He had scarcely finished giving his instructions when swift hoofs pounded up. Celestino Mireles burst in the door.

"General!" he cried, his dark eyes gleaming. "Zey come! Ze beeg gang we fight down zere!"

"About how many?" demanded Bob Pryor.

Mireles shrugged. "Two hundred, three—I could not count, but ees same bunch. Pronto!"

The Rio Kid, who had been taking no unnecessary chances after the deadly trap into which he had ridden on his trip with the posse, had told the loyal Mexican to stay out and keep a sharp eye on the back trail, just in case.

"Guns loaded and ready, boys!" snapped the Rio Kid. His swift fingers felt his own Colts in their oiled, supple holsters. "Keep it quiet, now. We'll catch 'em as they come across the creek. Get to the bank and take what cover yuh find!"

# CHAPTER XI

## *Spy*

☐ Bob Pryor was pleased. He had not expected to get a
crack at the Henry-Owens gang so soon but here they
came, riding straight into his guns. The stars were bright
and horsemen would loom against the sky.

"C'mon, Frenchy!" he called. "I'll give yuh a grand-
stand seat."

"J-just a sec," stammered Dupuy. "I'll be with you."

The settlers were scattering, moving toward the bank
of the stream. The Rio Kid turned at the door, to wait for
his supposed ally. He was surprised at the chalkiness of
Frenchy's cheeks, over the sharp-pointed little goatee,
and saw that the fellow's slim hand was shaking as he
pulled on his coat.

"Is he yeller?" wondered Pryor.

Dupuy had put up some big talk. But now that his
chance had come to help the Lane folks he was slow
about it. The Rio Kid hated a coward, and if Dupuy
were one he wanted to find out about it before he went
any farther with the friendship. He had no inkling as yet
that Frenchy was a spy, a spy for the very man he was
seeking.

"Hustle up," he said. "I'm in a hurry."

Frenchy came walking out, rather unsteadily. His face was working with nervousness.

"Got yore gun?" asked the Rio Kid.

"Yes—in my pocket."

"Let's go, then. We'll want to be in the thick of it."

He kept the little gambler at his side as they made for the bulge of the creek bank. The stream was silver in the night light, its low sound drowning out nearby slight noises.

The Rio Kid chose a rock that bulged up and would offer some shelter from massed lead when it drove from the opposite bank. Dupuy crouched beside him, his teeth chattering.

Ears wide and strained, the Rio Kid caught a new note in the wilderness, the faint pounding of many hoofs. It came rapidly nearer and soon his keen eyes could make out the dark masses of horsemen headed toward the crossing that led to the new settlement.

They were coming fast, full-tilt, reckless of discovery.

Not a sound came from the line of farmers, waiting with their cocked rifles and shotguns. The Rio Kid peeked over his rock, watching the van of the raiders splash down the other side into the shallows, while the great gang of gunnies closed up.

When the first contingent was halfway across, the Rio Kid threw up his pistols.

"Now!" he shouted in a stentorian voice.

He raised his thumbs and the Colts roared death and flame. The leading riders fell from their saddles into the icy water. Down the line, Lane and his men pulled triggers and the volley tore into the massed thieves.

Curses of fury and the blasting reply of the killers started. The Rio Kid and his fighters were outnumbered five to one but they had the advantage of cover, of surprise, of being on foot.

Though not expert shots, most of the farmers could handle guns and the mass of the oncoming men was so wide, they were so close together, that they could not be missed.

In the creek bed, pandemonium raged, as men sought to whirl their horses and retreat before the withering fire of the Rio Kid and the outraged farmers. Those behind were pushing ahead. The wings split off, terrified mustangs fighting the bit, and dashing through the shallows along the gauntlet of the settlers' muzzles.

Hot in the fight, the Rio Kid was concentrating upon picking off bandits. He saw the main body of them easing down the stream, forced that way by the bullets tearing in their front and flanks. Leaping up, he started after them to make every shot count.

Suddenly he remembered Dupuy. The little man had remained crouched, head down, pressed to the frozen earth, in the thick of the fight, with the rock sheltering him.

"Dupuy!" he shouted, his officer's voice carrying over the battle din. "Get yore guns goin', blast yuh!"

The hot blood of the fighting man, the true soldier, was high in his swiftly beating heart, but his nerves and reactions were as sure and cool as normal. He hated a coward, and Frenchy—

Suddenly the little man jumped up while wild bullets smashed the rocks about him, and ran around the other side, bent low.

The Rio Kid was surprised. Dupuy was running into the face of the enemy across the stream!

"Come back!" he began, but Frenchy was waist deep in the water now.

A dozen of the rustlers were over there, some forced up the bank by the crush in the center. Seeing Dupuy coming over, they turned their guns on him.

The Rio Kid saw the flare of their guns as they swung on Dupuy. Thinking to save the little man who, he decided, must have lost his head in the hysteria of fear the battle had thrown him into Pryor let go at them to cover Frenchy, yelling at Dupuy to return to the near shore.

Spurts of water close about the moving head and shoulders showed how close the slugs were.

"Everts—Dutch!" Dupuy began screaming in a high-pitched, fear-laden voice. "Boys, it's Dupuy! Don't shoot me—don't shoot me! Everts—Dutch—call them off!"

"Hey, Frenchy!" bellowed a dark figure from the other bank. "What in creation's up?"

Slugs raged back and forth over the water. A dozen of the gunmen were dead while others had felt the hot lead of the settlers. Enthusiasm for a frontal attack rapidly evaporated, none desiring to cross the open space of the creek in the face of such withering fire.

The Rio Kid, astounded by what he heard Dupuy calling, stared through the gloom as Dupuy splashed into the shallows and clawed at a horseman's stirrups, begging to be taken up.

"Everts!" he thought.

Again he threw up his revolver to shoot, running after Dupuy. A bullet hit him in the left forearm, spinning him around, and he knew he missed his aim for Dupuy was able to jump up behind one of the horse thieves.

They were concentrating on the Rio Kid, and he dropped behind some rocks.

In a few moments, the riders, one carrying Dupuy clinging to him, were in the fringe of brush out of sight.

Terrible thoughts raced through the Rio Kid's brain. Could the man he had been seeking, Valentine Everts, the crooked contractor, actually be riding with Dutch Henry's gang? And Dupuy! Besides being a coward, the little man obviously was a spy, connected with the horse thieves.

He shook his head, unable to connect all this up at the moment, in the hot battle. The wound had shocked him and blood trickled warm down his hand that was stiffening in the cold.

"I need Dupuy," he muttered, "to explain that Everts business! Glad I didn't kill him."

"There they go!" Norton Lane, heading his men in the center, roared with triumph.

The rustlers had turned and were riding away at top speed, leaving their dead behind them. Bodies lay in the shallows of the creek, with the current rippling over them. More dead were curled up on the bank.

Flashing guns snarled back at the victorious Lanetown contingent, more of whom, hearing the heavy shooting, had come riding up from outlying points.

The Rio Kid, injured, but pulling himself together, speeded the killers on their way as they retreated into the darkness of the cold prairie. They kept shooting until the horse thieves' replies were pinpoints in the night.

With pickets set out then, like the careful commander that he was, the Rio Kid gathered his friends together after the clean-up of the battlefield. Wounded must be quickly wrapped against the cold, and their hurts treated.

Lanetown had several men with bullet tears and two had died, but the horse thieves had lost fifteen men, and many more were wounded.

The settlers remained on the alert through the night, but the horse thieves evidently had had a bellyful of the kind of reception planned by the Rio Kid.

The dawn broke with an overcast sky. It looked as though it might snow.

Pryor's arm wound was not serious, but he had lost some blood. Mireles, with a painful crease on one brown, lean cheek, where a rustler bullet had nearly finished him, was content so long as he was with his friend.

The Rio Kid spoke to Norton Lane and his aides.

"Yuh can't keep this up forever," Pryor declared. "That passel of wolves will have to be exterminated. It's up to the Law of the county, and that means Bat Masterson. He'll need to know about this last night's business, and how many of 'em there are. I better ride to Dodge on the double and talk to him. In the meantime, hold yore people in here, close together, Lane, so's they can be defended easier. And keep sentries out from dark till dawn, savvy? Soon as Bat and me are organized, we'll be along and after those skunks."

Norton Lane nodded. "We're shore obliged to you, Rio Kid. You've saved us, in more than one way. But I don't understand why those outlaws are so furious at us."

"I don't either—yet," replied Pryor. "But I mean to find out. If I get my hands on Frenchy Dupuy—"

He broke off with a shrug. He preferred deeds to boasts. To himself he kept the startling clue which Dupuy had let slip in his lather of fright the night before, concerning Valentine Everts.

"Could it be," he mused, "that they're comin' after these folks just to get me?"

It seemed an elaborate set-up for the purpose of killing a single enemy, the Rio Kid. Everts might do it, to insure his own hide against the vengeance of the Rio Kid. Frenchy Dupuy undoubtedly had reported to Everts that the Rio Kid was hunting the thieving contractor, and Pryor guessed that Dupuy had been sticking close to him to inform Everts of every move he made.

But Dutch Henry and Tom Owens would scarcely throw their powerful gangs into such a dangerous game without at least the promise of remuneration. It cost money to run such an organization.

However, he knew his first move must be to hurry to Dodge City and tell Bat Masterson of the forces they were against. They were still in the vicinity and their trail might be picked up afresh when Bat had his army ready to ride.

Repeating his warning to Lane never to relax vigilance for a moment, the Rio Kid saddled up and, with Mireles at his side, took the shortest line for Dodge.

## CHAPTER XII

## *Lore of a Marshal*

☐ Lights were twinkling on as the Rio Kid and Celestino crossed the Santa Fe tracks and clattered along Front Street.

But Bat Masterson was in Dog Kelley's place, having a drink before supper. He greeted the Rio Kid jovially, and then listened, face grave, to Pryor's report.

"Blast them!" he growled. "Why should they hit those pore folks out there? Dutch has run off hosses all over the Frontier, but this is the worst yet. I've called in men for deputies but it takes a few days to make such a large force ready. I'll trail them to the Mexican border if I have to, and to tarnation with the county line!"

"Let's hope they don't split up," the Rio Kid replied.

"Howdy, Rio Kid!" a man sang out behind him.

It was Dave Garrett. Pryor shook hands, staring at the young farmer curiously. Garrett still wore range clothing, and the two new six-shooters whose walnut stocks had hardly been touched by sweat or grease, rode in stiff-looking holsters at his burly hips. On his handsome head a black felt with a narrow brim was strapped tight.

His face was smooth-shaven and glowed with health. He seemed to be a good deal happier than when the Rio Kid had last seen him.

However, it was not any of that which intrigued the Rio Kid so much as it was the badge pinned over Garrett's heart. It read:

DEPUTY MARSHAL
DODGE CITY, KAN.

He caught Bat Masterson's eye for an instant and read a volume in it. A faint line showed between the cold blue orbs of the famous Ford County sheriff.

"Have a drink, Dave," the Rio Kid cried.

"Thanks, I will."

Garrett stepped up and put a booted foot on the rail. Behind his back, Bat winked at the Rio Kid, who was still puzzled.

Then Dog Kelley strolled over and greeted Pryor, making a fuss over him. The jovial mayor was delighted to see the Rio Kid. He was not the kind who forgot a friend.

"I see yuh've taken Garrett on, Dog," remarked the Rio Kid casually, as he fingered his whiskey glass.

"Oh, shore!" shouted Kelley. "That was the least I could do for a pard of yores, Rio Kid." He beamed his good-natured pleasure at having done a favor for Pryor.

"How yuh gettin' on, Dave?" asked the Rio Kid.

"Fine!" replied Garrett.

A large man in his shirtsleeves, wearing a green eye-shade, stepped to the center of the place.

"Qui-et!" he bellowed.

The buzz of talk ceased and the announcer continued in his belligerent manner:

"Yuh'll now be favored with a song by the silver-tongued canary of Dodge, Miss Alice Lane, exclusive with Kelley's Place, the greatest on the Frontier. If anybody so much as winks in the next five minutes he'll be dealt with plenty—savvy?"

For a moment he scowled, hunting with his eyes for possible troublemakers, then bowed and retired.

The men strung along the bar turned so they could see the pretty girl standing in the Annex by the piano and violin. Wide doors were open so they could look through from the saloon.

Alice's full, natural voice rose in song:

Oh don't you remember sweet Alice, Ben Bolt,
Sweet Alice, with hair so brown?
She wept with delight when you gave her a smile,
And trembled with fear at your frown.

A man slouched at a nearby table put his head down on his arms and began sobbing in maudlin nostalgia as the refrain tore his heart.

"He's been tankin' up since before breakfast," growled Dog Kelley. "If he don't restrain his grief like a gent I'll have to bounce him out."

The second verse moved the man to high-pitched yowls of self-pity. The man in the eyeshade seized him by the scruff of the neck, dragged him protesting to the batwings and threw him out with a professional touch, dusting off his hands at the finish.

After the girl had completed her song, the Rio Kid and Dave Garrett went to her. She was happy to see Pryor, and smiled on Garrett, who seemed to be more in her favor.

"How are Mother and Dad?" she asked the Rio Kid. "You've seen them?"

"Yeah, Alice, I was there. Just got back. No doubt yuh heard how we chased the gang that hit Lanetown? Well, they come back, more of 'em, and we had a little fight."

Her eyes grew anxious. "They—Mother and Dad aren't hurt, are they?"

"No. But it was a battle and some men yuh know were hit."

Garrett frowned. He looked at the Rio Kid, then at the girl. He did not want to leave Alice, but it was plain he was deliberating on returning to help his friends.

No one had seen Frenchy Dupuy. The little man knew better than to return to Dodge, after he had given himself away in the panic of the battle.

Dave Garrett was going on patrol, as the evening

85

began to warm up Dodge. Texas men from the blanket camps were drifting in, their tempers frayed with boredom and inaction. The Civil War still rankled in many of their hearts, too, though it was twelve years gone. They were the sons of the South, here in what was almost—to them—an alien land.

The Rio Kid returned to Masterson, to discuss the coming campaign after the Henry-Owens gang. He had only just begun to talk when a man's voice sang out behind him:

"Well, if it ain't the Rio Kid!"

Pryor swung. A lean, smiling-faced man was coming toward him with outstretched hand. There was a laugh in his blue eyes.

"Billy Tilghman! Ain't see yuh since Salt Lake City!"

"Billy's my under-sheriff in the county," Bat said.

"Yeah, I been down in the Panhandle huntin' a killer," Tilghman said.

"Did yuh find him?"

"When yuh send Billy after a man," remarked Masterson, "yuh only need to ask, did he walk or was he carried?"

Already young Billy Tilghman was being called "Uncle." He was a natural law officer, cool and fast when necessary. Everybody liked him.

When the Rio Kid left Tilghman and Masterson later, he went outside into the swirling, crowded street. He wanted a word with Dave Garrett. He found Dave, whom Dog Kelley, through a mistaken act of kindness, had appointed a deputy marshal on the Dodge City police force, leaning with his back to a wall, close to a narrow alley.

"Dave, will yuh take some advice from a friend?" the Rio Kid asked.

"Sure, sure!"

"Supple up them holsters," advised the Rio Kid. "Yuh can rub saddle oil in 'em twice a day and get 'em so's they won't drag when yuh draw. Yuh been practicin' pullin' yore gun?"

"Yes, sir. Wyatt Earp showed me." Garrett made a draw which was fast, but not quite what it should be. "I had to knock a cowboy out the other night," Dave went on seriously. "Didn't like to hurt him, but he made me."

"I see."

The Rio Kid rolled himself a smoke, lighted up. Past them flowed the panorama of Dodge, the stalking buffalo hunters, the riding, wild Texas men from the Trail, and riffraff of the Frontier in every shape and dress. Wagons and buggies cluttered the curbs, while saddled horses stood at the hitch-racks by the hundreds. Lights were on and at the Opera House a bill poster announced that John Drew was the current attraction.

From the south, by way of the toll bridge over the Arkansas, came a band of hard-riding Texas cowboys. They galloped full-tilt across the Santa Fe tracks, whooping the Rebel yell shrilly. Most of them had already had a few drinks on the way in from their camp, and were in the usual belligerent mood.

Gun-toting, except by officers of the law, was forbidden above the deadline, the railroad. Nevertheless the cowmen drew their six-shooters and began firing into the air, punctuating the explosions with their sharp cries.

"That's me," Garrett said, and started across to intercept them, warn them about the shooting.

The Rio Kid tagged behind, watching Garrett in action.

"Say, gents," Garrett said, planting himself in front of the cowboys' leader, "you'll have to check your guns at the nearest saloon. No gun-carryin' in Dodge."

"Get out of the way, you!" the Texas man shouted.

"Now wait!" Garrett cried. "Let's talk it over, boys. No sense in buckin' the law, is there?"

The cowboy raised his quirt and slashed at Garrett's eyes. A red welt appeared on Dave's bronzed cheek. The other cowboys laughed and dug in their spurs, but the Rio Kid sprang in, seized the leader's wrist and yanked him out of the saddle.

The big Texan sprawled in the dust. His face was crimson as he rolled over and came up on one knee, his hand dropping to his Colt.

Each move the Rio Kid made was precise, unerring. He let the cowboy start to draw, then beat him to it, his

Colt flashing into his hand with the speed of legerdemain.

"Dave—don't shoot!" he ordered, as he saw Garrett, from the corner of one eye, drag his gun from its stiff holster.

An instant-flash later, the Rio Kid's heavy pistol barrel clonked on the Texan's head. The troublemaker folded up in the dust at Pryor's feet. The Rio Kid looked at the mounted gang.

"All right, boys," he said coolly, seeking each man's eyes, "check yore hoglegs like the marshal says and yuh can bail out yore friend for twenty-five dollars in the mornin'."

They swore about it, but split up and dismounted, entering various saloons.

"Pick him up," ordered Pryor.

Dave Garrett shouldered the fellow Pryor had buffaloed and started for the calaboose, two blocks away. The Rio Kid walked beside him.

"There was no use to kill him and if yuh'd shot yuh'd have had to, Dave. He's full of red-eye, but he's not the kind who needs lead. It would have meant a feud with the other Texans camped outside."

Garrett nodded. "I savvy."

The prisoner was deposited in a cell, and the two went back on patrol.

"On the other hand," continued the Rio Kid, going on with a lesson he hoped Garrett would take to heart, "yuh couldn't let him get away with quirtin' yuh. They'da thought they could pull anything they wanted in Dodge, and it would have got to be a landslide that nothin' could check, savvy?"

Garrett blinked. "Why, I reckon so."

"Some men yuh got to shoot and when yuh do, shoot to kill."

The Rio Kid did his best to impart to Dave the lore of the Western marshal. Pryor had on several occasions undertaken such work in the wild, hard-fighting Frontier settlements.

After a time he left Garrett and went inside for a drink. It was Saturday night, and Dodge simply howled louder and louder while fun and fury grew to maniacal proportions, unbelievable in its scope. The South Side, of course, beyond the pale, was even worse than north of the tracks.

# CHAPTER XIII

## *No Man for a Killing*

☐ Uneasy about Garrett, the Rio Kid went out later and stood in the shadows of an awning, watching the young marshal parade the edge of the plaza to which he was assigned. From it he could watch the crowded sidewalk and the entrances to the saloons and gambling houses.

A man staggered by him, brushing his arm. The light shaft from a nearby window fell on the reddened, bewhiskered face. Little pig eyes, gleaming with red hate, showed over a swollen, curved nose. Tobacco juice had stained his slit of a mouth and the beard around it. His coat was unbuttoned, and the Rio Kid saw the glint of a pistol beneath it.

He was, the Rio Kid saw instantly, one of the riffraff the Frontier was often spewing forth—a gunman, no doubt a killer. He ducked under the hitch-rack and started across the road. Suddenly he let out a curse and seized a small youth by the scruff of the neck, jerking him around.

"There yuh are, yuh little skunk!" he shouted, and began beating the boy unmercifully, knocking him down and kicking him in the stomach.

Dave Garrett dashed over.

"Hey—leave him alone! He's too little for yuh to belt thataway!"

The fellow left off his cruel sport and turned on Garrett, his small, piggish eyes narrowing.

"What's that?" he said mildly.

Garrett faced him, frowning. "I say he's too little for yuh to beat up. Only a kid."

"He's a little rat," the red-eyed man snarled, his lips twisting. "I told him to bring me some money and he ain't done it."

"Now listen," Garrett begged. "Go on home and sleep off your likker. I don't want trouble with you, but—"

"Yuh threatenin' me?"

Garrett braced himself. His slow temper was rising.

"I am if you don't behave yourself. G'wan, now."

He seized the burly, ugly man by the shoulder and flung him toward the sidewalk. The man staggered but caught himself. He began walking off as though the episode were finished, while Garrett turned to the cowering boy.

But the instant Dave Garrett's eyes were off the bearded fellow, the man whipped the pistol from under his coat, raised it and fired.

The Rio Kid saw the killer's slug kick up the dirt a yard from Garrett's foot.

His own pistol had pushed against his steady hand a breath ahead of the gunman's. He had known, intuitively, that the ruffian was going to pull the trick and was in a killing mood. Pryor had been close enough to save Garrett from death.

Garrett swung, getting his Colt out and cocked, turned on the man who had sought to finish him off over the slightest of arguments. The pig-eyed devil was still up, gun in his hand, although his arm had begun to drop as the Rio Kid's skillfully placed bullet drilled his side, a move which had meant life instead of death for Garrett. His knees were buckling, and his bearded face contorted.

Garrett should have fired, to make certain of him, but did not when he saw his opponent was hit. But the Rio Kid knew what such a person was capable of doing in a last convulsive effort to take his enemy to death with him. The Kid raised his thumb a second time and finished the fellow off with a head shot. The Colt fell from the limp hand and the Border ruffian fell dead in the dust.

The boy the fellow had been beating got to his feet.

"Good," he said, and walked away.

The Rio Kid ducked under the hitch-rail and joined Garrett, who was staring down at the perforated bully.

"Dave, Dave!" he chided. "Couldn't yuh see he was that kind? Never argue with one if he gives yuh lip. Take away the gun he's shore to have hid on him and if he so much as bats an eyelid, shoot him dead."

Garrett shrugged. A silent crowd collected for a few minutes, staring at the crumpled mess in the gutter.

Wyatt Earp, lean and pantherish, a Colt with an extra long barrel at his sinewy hip, strolled over and joined the Rio Kid. There was a sly, amused gleam in Earp's fine, deep-set eyes.

"Hello, Mama," he said to Pryor.

The Rio Kid grinned. "Come along and let's have a drink on it, Wyatt. I need one."

The tall chief marshal of Dodge swung into step beside the Rio Kid.

"I been wet-nursin' that lad myself ever since Dog Kelley made me take him on as a deputy," he remarked musingly. "Rio Kid, he'll never make a peace officer. He just don't savvy when to shoot. He's slow, but it ain't so much that and lack of experience—he'll soon speed up and learn the tricks of the trade with practice—but he's too blamed kind-hearted and hates to kill a man, no matter how much said hombre might need it. Yuh'll see. Tomorrer he'll worry all day over that dead skunk, who ought to have had room made for him in Boot Hill long ago. He was one of Tom Owens' old bunch of hoss thieves and I was just waitin' for a crack at him if he so much as raised an eyebrow."

"Yuh're right, Wyatt," agreed the Rio Kid. "I watched Dave this evening and he'll never make a good marshal. It ain't in him. Mebbe he's too good-hearted, as yuh say. I'm afraid he'll go the same route Ed Masterson did."

"Me, too. In fact, I'll lay yuh a hunderd to one that

92

Garrett don't last out the week, countin' next Saturday night, 'less you foller him around and do his shootin' for him."

"That would be takin' my money!" The Rio Kid laughed. "But jokin' aside, Wyatt, Garrett's too decent a man to have some no-good sidewinder plug him full of lead while Dave's tryin' to make him see the light of reason."

That's my point, Rio Kid. That little singer, Alice Lane, in Kelley's, is the reason for it, I believe. Garrett can't keep away from her. It's like a moth flittin' close to a lamp flame and gettin' burnt to death. I've talked some to him and he claims he wants to be like you."

Earp was a shrewd judge of human nature. He cast a sidelong glance at the Rio Kid to make sure that Pryor understood what he was saying behind the actual sentences he spoke. Wyatt Earp was, as a rule, a man of few words, but now he was sufficiently disturbed to talk earnestly for some time concerning Dave.

"He's a nice young feller. That's why I'd hate to have to officiate at his burial."

"Farmin' is his line." The Rio Kid nodded. But he's been drawn to Dodge. I'm goin' to talk to Kelley."

"Garrett won't want to leave that girl—yuh'll see," Earp prophesied.

They went into the crowded saloon and all eyes turned on the two famous fighting men, Wyatt Earp and the Rio Kid, both known from Border to Border as square-shooters and splendid officers.

After wetting their whistles, Earp inquired:

"How yuh mean to go about gettin' Dave Garrett to go back to farmin'?"

The Rio Kid set down his empty glass.

"Wait'll I see Dog Kelley. There he is, in the back."

Earp trailed slowly after his friend. Mayor Kelley was sitting at a table, with some women friends, but at the Rio Kid's approach, he glanced up and grinned. A wink brought him to Pryor.

"I got another favor to ask you, Dog," said the Rio Kid.

"What is it?" Kelley inquired.

"Fire Dave Garrett off the police force."

Dog Kelley blinked and frowned.

"But—why, the boy's a friend of yores, Rio Kid. That's why, when he begged me to give him a chance, I told Wyatt to take him on. Earp didn't want to, said he was too green, but he did it to oblige me."

"That's why I want yuh to take away his badge," said Bob Pryor. "He ain't the type, Dog."

Kelley looked mournful. "I savvy," he said at last. "He'll go the way Ed did. That was my fault, and I'll never forgive myself for it. All right. I'll fire Garrett."

"Give him another job, if yuh want, dealin' faro or somethin'. But don't leave him set up as a target. It's my fault as much as yores."

"How do yuh mean?"

The Rio Kid shrugged. He was thinking that it was he who had been responsible for these two young people being uprooted, brought to Dodge. Alice's admiration for him had forced Garrett to give up his work and try to imitate the gun-fighter.

Both of them had been drawn into the maelstrom of the cowtown capitol and there was no saying what would be the end.

In the meantime, the evil crew of gunmen, commanded by Dutch Henry and Tom Owens, and with Valentine Everts supplying the brains for the job they had in hand, had ridden south after the attack on Lanetown which the Rio Kid had so skillfully repelled, with the aid of the settlers.

The leaders were in a black mood of fury at the defeat, at loss of so many fighters. Behind them came the rank and file, grumbling and cursing, many of them nursing bullet wounds received in the night fray.

"Curse yore hide, Dupuy," snarled Dutch Henry, swinging in his leather to swear at the little man who rode close to Everts, "why didn't yuh give us a yell 'fore we run into that trap? A warnin' would have saved a lot of woe."

Dupuy was still shaking from the narrow squeak.

"He would have shot me dead," he growled. "The Rio Kid would have killed me, Henry, if I'd tried it."

"Huh!" Dutch said belligerently. "Small loss."

Everts took the little spy's part, however.

"Let him alone, Dutch. He never claimed to be a fightin' man, did he? That ain't his line. And the Rio Kid's exceptional."

"Wait'll I come face to face with him next," boasted Dutch Henry, "and I'll show yuh how exceptional he is, Everts. I'll blow his stummick through his back."

"Huh!" grunted Everts. "I hope you do, Dutch. But don't waste any time about it."

"What now?" Owens broke in impatiently. "Are we givin' up?"

"Like sin," replied Henry. "We've put too much in this to quit."

Everts nodded.

"News of the fight'll be sent to Dodge at once. That means that inside of two or three days, at the most, Bat Masterson will have reinforcements out here and it'll be all the tougher. We ought to hit again, before they come."

"The men are wore out," objected Dutch Henry. "They got to rest."

"Let 'em have a drink instead. They can snooze when we hit the hills."

"What hills?"

"As soon as we're well below the settlement," said Everts, "we'll swing west and cross the creek. We can get up behind the town by enterin' the hills. We'll lie up there till dark tomorrow and try again."

"But it'll have to be easier than it was tonight, Everts," Henry objected. "Nobody wants to commit suicide."

"I have an idea," said Everts, and hastily outlined it.

Following Everts' orders, the big crew of gunmen turned and made their way over the icy creek. Dawn found them back in the low hills to the west of Lanetown, hiding in the scrub brush and tall grass that covered the section.

They could look down from the heights and see, in the distance, the smoke of the settlement.

The sun warmed them sufficiently so they could sleep, wrapped in their blankets, lying close together for what animal heat their bodies afforded.

# CHAPTER XIV

## *Siege*

☐ Night had fallen when Everts and Dutch Henry, with several picked men, rode on ahead, while Tom Owens fetched the main part of the gang on their trail. It was around midnight when they dismounted. Then they could see the dark shapes of the settlement's huts on the creek bank.

This time they were on the same side of the creek as the homes, and did not have to cross the stream. Everts, moving in the lead with an Indian's stealth, and with Dutch Henry closely following, crept closer and closer. Not far away a horseman was slowly patroling, watching for trouble, though his main interest was focused on the road which came in over the creek ford.

Everts and his companion finally reached the rear of a big wooden barn in which hay and wagons were stored. They managed to get a window open at the back and climbed in. Within a few minutes they emerged and retreated as silently as they had come.

Owens had arrived with the huge bunch of killers whose guns were loaded and ready for the slaughter.

As Everts remounted and turned to look, he could see a mounting red glow from the barn, which Henry and he had set afire. It was catching rapidly and soon the flames

97

burst through the thin roof. The settlers, roused from their sleep by the guards, came hurrying out to douse the fire.

"Spread out and drive in full-speed!" ordered Everts. "They'll be busy with the fire. They've got a bucket line to the creek already, and they'll have put down their guns to handle the pails."

Norton Lane and his friends reacted just as Everts had figured they would. The sudden fire was thought to be accidental, as no alarm had come from the sentries. The settlers left their rifles and shotguns behind the several big cabins where they had been sleeping, their chief thought to check the flames and prevent any spread to the other structures.

And at this moment, the terrible army of killers came sweeping in. The thud of hoofs was drowned by the shouts of the firefighters.

"Let 'em have it!" roared Val Everts.

A fusillade caught the Lanetown men out in the open, against the red glow of the burning barn. Several went down, some never to rise again, while wounded began crawling painfully to shelter, with friends seeking to assist them.

*Bang! Bang-Bang!* The one-two danger signal told that the rustlers were at hand.

Confusion struck the settlers, for the surprise was complete. Norton Lane, close to the burning barn, sprang to action, seeking to rally his fighters. He whipped a pistol from a holster at his hip, and emptied it at the line of riders that tore down upon them.

"Inside—take to the loopholes, boys!" Lane yelled.

Pails were dropped and the bucket line streaked for the safety of the cabins. Behind their walls they might resume their fire at the enemy.

Lane staggered back, as the heavy roar of exploding shells deafened the ears. He went down, but came up on his knees, got to his feet, nearly fell again, but began hopping on one leg.

In the moment he had stopped there to shoot, his startled men had run around the burning building. Some of them realized he was not with them and started back, calling to him.

But the rustlers already were within the main settlement, speeding in circles among the houses, firing at every moving thing. Confusion dominated Lanetown. By sheer force of gunfire the bandits forced the men inside, as they swore and whooped in their frenzy of victory.

In the ruby glow the scene was like some infernal nightmare as masked riders with bandannas drawn up to the snout, their eyes glinting with the lust of murder, rode like mad centaurs through Lanetown. They sent their bullets at everything that moved.

A couple more shacks started burning, as the stricken pioneers sought to pull themselves together for defense.

The rising light cast its rays high into the sky, tingeing the wind clouds. This gave the settlers in the windows and loopholes illumination by which to take aim. Their hands steadied on their weapons as they saw bandit after bandit fall from his saddle.

Stalwart hearts took fresh hope and fighting blood rose in the attacked pioneers. Their guns spat death at the enemy.

The rustlers did not like such fighting. When all had gone their way they had been lion-hearted, but with gun danger threatening them every instant now, they began to hunt the darker spots or keep the bulk of barns between themselves and the snarling muzzles of the pioneer guns. The three bandit chiefs, Dutch Henry, Owens and Everts, with their lieutenants sought in vain to drive their men in to put a finish to the fight.

"Where in creation is Norton Lane?" Ben McCrory cried, inside one of the buildings. "I ain't seen or heard him since the start of the fight."

"He was over at the burnin' barn, the last I seen him," a settler answered him.

When, presently, the volume of the shooting was not so heavy, they began calling to men holed up in other nearby cabins. No one had seen Lane since the start of the battle.

In one of the shacks, Mrs. Lane was helping to load guns and tend the injured. But she had no idea where her husband was, either, and was torn with an aching anxiety.

"They musta got Nort," McCrory muttered savagely, for Lane was his best friend as well as his leader.

The hours dragged on, with one wooden structure after another crashing into redhot ruins. The gang of night riders did not leave but remained within gunshot, throwing lead in at the settlers.

The pale dawn brought out the full details of the destruction wrought on Lanetown by the cruel Everts and his gunnies. Several barns and houses had been razed, were charred embers. The cold-stiffened corpses of rustlers and settlers who had given up their lives to protect their homes were stretched on the battleground. A dozen or more dead horses were scattered about.

A circle of death was around Lanetown, and inside the buildings the besieged waited, holding off the horde of killers.

Norton Lane had been given up for lost. . . .

In Dodge City, that Saturday night had been particularly hectic. Sunday came, cold and clear, but leaving each celebrant with a sickish feeling.

Dodge had a reputation to sustain, but sometimes overdid it, as now. Debris from the evening before littered the streets, and the saloons had not yet been cleaned of evidences of a riotous night.

On the South Side, across the Santa Fe tracks, three dead men, two of them Mexicans, were picked up, stiff as boards, and carted to Boot Hill, already filled to overflowing with such casualties. Guns had killed two, while the third had been done in with a knife. As was too often the case, no one knew who was responsible. Farther along the street a saloon had been set afire by some jovial patron, but water from the street barrels had put it out before it had spread.

Dodge had roared unceasingly until the icy fingers of dawn had checked the sport. Many had been wounded in fights. But that was forgotten now, for everybody was sleeping it off.

The Rio Kid got up around noon. He had taken little to drink during the evening, having spent his time watching Dave Garrett.

When he left the hayloft in which he had slept, he was cleaned up and his usual spruce self. He had something to eat with Mireles, then went to the little back room in Kelley's where Garrett lived.

He found Dave up, and on his bunk was a carpetbag into which the young man was packing his few belongings.

"Mornin', Dave."

Garrett nodded to him, but kept on with his packing. The Rio Kid stepped in, shut the wooden-slab door.

The young farmer had discarded his cowboy outfit, and now wore the clothing in which he had arrived in Dodge, his farmer's heavy clothing. He wore no deputy badge and the Rio Kid guessed that Dog Kelley had asked for it.

"Where yuh bound?" asked Pryor, slouching against the door frame.

"Home."

The Rio Kid felt sorry for the young fellow. He knew that Alice meant the world to Garrett.

"Yuh've quit the police force?"

"Yeah. Kelley asked for my star."

"I see." The Rio Kid frowned. "Dave," he went on in a moment, "that was my idea. I told him to do it. Earp agrees with me. We couldn't stand by and see yuh killed, as yuh woulda been if yuh'd kept on with the work. It's nothin' against yuh, that yuh ain't fitted for it. Sometimes I think a man who can't kill in cold blood is a sight better than one who can."

Garrett turned his blue eyes to the Rio Kid's.

"That's all right, Rio Kid. I savvied all along I wasn't the kind. But—" He broke off, with a shrug.

"I understand why yuh did it. But why not get a job at somethin' else if yuh have to be in Dodge? I'll see if someone won't take yuh on in a store or—"

Garrett shook his head.

"Dog Kelley offered me a dealer's job in the Alhambra. But— Well, Dodge ain't the place for me. I don't suit it and it don't suit me. I like farmin' and animals, and not this crazy city life, stayin' up all night while you ought to be sleepin'. Drinkin's no pleasure far as I'm concerned, at least not wallowin' in it. And I hate fightin' with every hombre who has a chip on his shoulder. I done the best I could, but I can't stick it out any longer."

"Yuh goin' back to Lanetown?"

Garrett nodded, finished stuffing his things into the carpetbag and snapped it shut.

"I'm goin' there and get my team of horses. I don't know as I'll stay long, though. Home means where you can plant things and grow 'em to me, Rio Kid."

"Dave," said the Rio Kid, "yuh got the right idea."

He held out his hand and the young giant took it.

"The best man won, I reckon," Garrett said deliberately.

The Rio Kid shook his head. But Dave Garrett clung to his notion.

Garrett rode out of Dodge City half an hour later, and headed west over the prairie toward Lanetown. . . .

At three o'clock in the afternoon, two cowboys who had been rounding up strays a couple of miles from a blanket camp on the plains southwest of Dodge, brought an unconscious man to Dodge City. Bat Masterson, thawing out the half-frozen, wounded fellow sent a messenger for the Rio Kid, who hurried to the City Hall. There he found Norton Lane lying on a pile of blankets. Bat Masterson, Wyatt Earp, Neal Brown and Billy Tilghman were around him.

"Lane!" exclaimed Pryor, kneeling to seize the man's hand. "What happened?"

"Attack," Lane whispered. "Bandits attacked—last night."

"He says it was mighty bad," growled Bat Masterson, chewing on his unlighted cigar. "A barn was set afire to draw the settlers out, then the gang swept in, shootin'. Lane was hit in the first volley, in the leg. It ain't busted, but the bone's bruised bad and he lost a lot of blood."

"Caught a horse—the rider was shot off," explained Norton Lane. "I saw they meant to stay there, and I couldn't get back in, so I come for help. They mean business this time. They'll stick there till they've killed us all!"

# CHAPTER XV

## *Maneuvers*

☐ Furious anger burned in Bob Pryor, and puzzlement as well. Why should they keep hitting Lanetown that way? For each time Everts and his cronies sent the gunmen in, they would lose fighters, and surely they could not afford such losses when no profit was in sight.

But he had no time to figure it out.

"Let's get goin', Bat, right now," he suggested.

"I'd like to," replied Bat, "but I ain't got all my men together. I'm expectin' a posse from Jetmore."

"The devil with that! I'm startin' now, Bat. I'll meet yuh in Lanetown."

"All right." Bat shrugged. "I can muster a hundred, I reckon, and I'll leave word for the others to follow."

As the Rio Kid swung, Alice Lane burst through the door and ran to her father's side. Tears stained her white cheeks as she took Lane's head in her arms and kissed him.

"Father—you're hurt! They just told me. Where's the doctor?"

"He's comin'," Bat Masterson answered her.

She was stricken with remorse at the sight of her injured father.

"I should have been there!" she cried.

Somehow, the news of the awful attack had reached her, and now her wounded father told her the worst. Moreover, her mother was still in Lanetown, and the grim attitude of the gun-fighters about the room told her that more danger threatened the settlement that was her home.

"Where is Dave Garrett?" she demanded. "Will someone please call him?"

Her words startled the Rio Kid. For instantly he remembered that Garrett was at that moment on his way to Lanetown. Without any warning that the killers were around the town, Dave Garrett would no doubt ride straight into the guns of the rustlers!

The Rio Kid drew Bat Masterson aside.

"Get every fightin' man yuh can dig up, Bat," he said hastily, "and start for Lanetown. If we hustle, we may make it in time. Them devils will savvy they can't stay around there too long, and if we wait, they may scatter. Then, too, they may pull some desperate trick to finish off them folks."

Bob Pryor hurried outside. He sent Celestino Mireles to the stable to saddle Saber and the Mexican's mount.

Dog Kelley was breakfasting when the Rio Kid burst in on him.

"Mornin'," began the mayor. "I done fired Dave Garrett as yuh asked—"

"Never mind that now, Dog!" The Rio Kid spoke hastily. "I need fighters, a big bunch of 'em, all yuh can spare! Lanetown's bein' attacked again by the Henry-Owens gang and even now it may be too late to save 'em. Norton Lane, Alice's father, was just brought in off the prairie, wounded. He says the bandits surprised the settlers and have 'em besieged in their homes."

Kelley sprang to his feet with an oath, his heavy figure shaking with rage.

"What the tarnation's the idea of it? Why can't that passel of polecats let them pore people alone?"

"I dunno—but I aim to find out. I'm ridin' on ahead to scout the ground. Bat says he'll foller."

"Blamed right he will! And I'll rout out every man who

104

can pull trigger in Dodge and dad-blast the jurisdiction! I'm with yuh!"

But the Rio Kid was gone. Within five minutes, with cartridge belts loaded, and two slings for his carbine suspended from the saddle-horn, he hit the trail for Lanetown. Mireles rode with him, but the speed of the dun was too much for the mustang the Mexican mounted to maintain. Before long, the young Mexican was left far behind. . . .

As the Rio Kid had feared, Dave Garrett did ride right into the ring of gunmen close about Lanetown. Expecting no such welcome, he came up after dark, having pressed straight over the plains to the settlement, and put his horse to the ford of the creek.

The first warning of anything amiss he had were clicking guns. Then dark figures sprang out, seized his startled mustang's reins, and pulled Garrett out of the saddle.

"Who is it?" he heard a gruff voice inquire.

"Strike a match!" someone else said. "It's dark as a stack of black cats."

"What's the idea?" Garrett demanded. "I'm no robber, boys. It's Dave, Dave Garrett."

A match flared and hard eyes peered at him.

"Why, so it is," a masked man jibed.

The houses were all dark, although it was early in the evening. The confused Garrett was aware that many armed men were about him, but instantly he knew that the same gang which had attacked Lanetown before was back.

Suddenly he opened his mouth and roared at the top of his lungs:

"Bandits! Look out, folks!"

Garrett, believing the bandits had just arrived, thought he was sacrificing himself to warn his friends. But the wolfish fellows about him laughed.

"Yuh're a leetle late with yore news, *amigo*," one of them drawled.

"What yuh up to?" Garrett demanded harshly. "Yuh're Dutch Henry's bunch, ain't yuh?"

He tried to fight off their restraining hands, but they had snatched the guns from his holsters and one of them hit him across the face. He pulled an arm loose and punched his tormentor but was thrown to earth, held down, and his wrists fastened behind him.

A knot of horsemen rode up and had a look at the captive. A tall masked devil dismounted and stood over Garrett.

"How soon will the Rio Kid and Masterson be here?" he demanded. "Do they savvy we've attacked?"

"How should I know?" snarled Garrett. The tall chief shrugged, and spurned him with a boot.

"Take him to the basin and let Dupuy guard him, boys. Come on, now! We've got to work fast. They can't have much more ammunition left in there."

"What yuh mean to do?" cried Dave.

"Shut up!" ordered the tall leader. And to his men: "Take him back and keep him quiet. We'll tend to him later. Maybe I can use him."

A cold chill touched Garrett. Not because his own life was threatened, but because he realized the ruthlessness of these men. They were not after loot, horses and personal belongings, but meant to kill. They were planning a wholesale murder of Lanetown folks.

"Yuh'll pay for this!" he promised furiously.

But they only beat him and, pulling him to his feet, dragged him down the creek bank to a small basin fringed with brush and rocks, which seemed to be their temporary headquarters in the field.

After Garrett's ankles were bound, he was flung to the hard earth, and could only lie there, helpless.

"Keep an eye on him, Frenchy," ordered the tall leader, and rode away with his men.

"Frenchy!" thought Garrett.

It was dim in there, and the cold soon permeated to his marrow. He could see the figure of a man muffled in a buffalo robe, squatted close by.

"Is that you, Dupuy?" he asked in a low voice.

"Yeah, it's me. Yuh run yore head into the trap, Garrett. Where's that cursed Rio Kid?"

"I dunno. I'm surprised you're in on this, Frenchy. I thought you was a friend of the Rio Kid's."

Frenchy Dupuy cursed viciously. "The coyotes'll soon be cleanin' his bones," he snarled.

"What's the idea? What's it all about? Why are you fellers so set on killin' us all?"

But Dupuy just shook his head. . . .

To the captive, the minutes dragged like so many tortuous hours.

Suddenly gunfire started over in the little clump of buildings, and the hoarse shouts of the criminal gang. A red glow rose into the sky.

Frenchy Dupuy, huddled under his thick buffalo hide, stared at the scene across the silvery stream. Flashes from the defenders' rifles showed from loops and windows. Dupuy's teeth began to chatter.

From where Garrett lay he could only hear the fighting. But one thing he did see. His eyes, rolling up, saw a man's head and Stetson silhouetted for an instant against the sky on the rim of the little basin, away from the creek and Lanetown. It was gone so quickly that Garrett thought he might have imagined it. Also, it might only be another of the killers, but—a thin thread of hope lifted his spirits.

Dupuy was gazing at Lanetown. A soft brushing sound close to Garrett's head sent the young farmer's glance that way. Dupuy's teeth were rattling, and also with his ears keened for the crackling shots he did not hear anything close by.

A wraith flitted through the darkness, low down like a stalking panther, toward Frenchy Dupuy. There was a dull, muffled thud, and Dupuy crunched up in the buffalo robe.

The ghostlike assailant turned quickly to Garrett, kneeling by him.

"Dave!" he whispered.

"Ssh, Dave!" breathed Bob Pryor.

His knife cut the rawhide lashings on Garrett's wrists and ankles. Then the Rio Kid used the cords to fasten Frenchy Dupuy. He took the precaution of gagging

Dupuy as well, and hoisted the little spy to his shoulder.

"C'mon, Garrett!" he whispered. "No time to talk here."

They went up the sliding bank and, keeping low, retreated over the plain. They could see the flashing guns and hear the reports of the weapons back over the creek in Lanetown.

"Listen, Rio Kid!" Garrett said urgently. "Them skunks mean to wipe out my friends. They're tryin' to draw their ammunition out and then they'll slaughter 'em. We got to go for help. Lemme ride!"

"Help's comin'," Pryor said grimly. "I rode on ahead, Dave."

They paused for breath and to reconnoiter, squatted in a buffalo wallow below the level of the plain.

"I need Dupuy," the Rio Kid said. "I was mighty glad to see him tonight."

" 'Twas like magic, you showin' up when yuh did," Garrett said admiringly. "I thought I was a goner."

"I was only three hours or so behind yuh, Dave," explained the Rio Kid. "I nearly caught up with yuh, to warn yuh, but dark fell and I had to slow some. I hid Saber back in a dry wash and slid up afoot. I heard 'em when they grabbed yuh, and watched my chance."

It sounded simple, the way the Rio Kid told it, but Garrett knew enough about scouting to realize that it had called for the most consummate skill and finesse. And such icy nerve was possessed by only a few men—men like Bob Pryor.

"Then you savvied the rustlers were here?"

"Yeah. Norton Lane rode to Dodge. He'd been wounded by 'em. He was comin' for help but got off the trail and some cowboys fetched him in. Yuh'd already gone. Lane warned us of the new attack." The Rio Kid paused and peered over the edge of the wallow. "Huh! The main gang's here, no doubt of it. I wonder if they expect a posse's comin' after 'em?"

"I think they do."

"I'm afraid they'll scatter, 'fore we can hit 'em right," Pryor said grimly.

"I hope the ammunition of our folks holds out," Garrett said soberly. "They didn't have so all-fired much of it."

The whispers of the two men were almost drowned out in the din. For, whooping, shooting at the windows of the besieged settler town, the outlaw gang made the night hideous.

Consciousness began to return to Frenchy Dupuy. He began whimpering under his gag, twitching a bit. He was coming back to terrified life.

"I've got to go in there and keep checkin' up, so's I can tell Bat what's what when he gets here, Dave," Pryor said rapidly. "You take charge of Frenchy and don't let him get away. I need him, I told yuh. I've got a score to settle with Dupuy's boss, who's also ridin' with Dutch Henry and his bunch. No time to palaver now, and Dupuy's groggy, anyhow."

"I'd enjoy goin' after them polecats," growled Garrett. "But I'll do whatever you say."

"Yuh'll have a chance, I guarantee," the Rio Kid promised grimly.

He gave a low whistle and out of the gloom slid Celestino Mireles, leading three horses. They had picked up a runaway from the Lanetown affray before dark, on their way over.

"Here's Garrett," the Rio Kid told his comrade, "and I captured Dupuy. Give Dave that spare hoss and keep Saber. Sling Dupuy over in front of yuh, Dave, and head straight back for Dodge. Yuh'll meet Bat Masterson and his men 'fore long. Give Bat my message, now."

He was careful to repeat his instructions, and made Garrett repeat them. Then he started Garrett, with Dupuy a limp, panic-stricken pack before him, away in the darkness.

The Mexican had charge of Saber, the Rio Kid's dun, who was trained to keep quiet, to fight when ordered, and to come at his rider's signal.

# CHAPTER XVI

## *Hare and Hounds*

☐ Quietly flitting back toward the creek, the Rio Kid again went down into the basin where he had captured Dupuy. It was clear of the enemy, but as he crouched near the dark bulk of the heavy buffalo robe which had shielded Frenchy Dupuy, some horsemen rode up and dismounted. Seeing the Rio Kid's crouched figure in the gloom, the rider in the lead called:

"That you, Frenchy? Where's the boss?"

Gunshots from across the creek rose on the crisp air.

"Over there," the Rio Kid growled in a muffled voice.

"Well, go get him and tell him we got enough stuff to blow ten towns like this here one off the map. We stole some from the railroad contractors' camp or we wouldn'ta made it so soon."

The riders apparently were pleased with themselves, judging by their hoarse chuckles. But they were also tired from a swift, long ride back with the explosives. There were four of them and each had two large cans of blasting powder balanced at his saddle-horn.

The Rio Kid had to think fast. So that was what Everts and Dutch Henry meant to do! Figuring they must finish Lanetown before the posse arrived, they had sent for explosives and fuses. With proper handling, crude bombs

110

tossed at the buildings would blow the unlucky farmers out of the homes that were their forts.

The Rio Kid was here alone. And at any moment a large contingent of the enemy might appear at the basin. Once in their hands, nothing could prevent the massacre of the settlers of Lanetown.

In a flash, he had the answer, the only one. The quartet of bandits were bunched together as they started with the cans of high-explosive toward the spot where the Rio Kid squatted. He drew both Colts, cocked them.

"Hold where yuh are, gents!" he ordered. "One move and I'll shoot!"

Consternation seized them.

"Why—that ain't Dupuy!" choked one of the riders.

"Put that stuff down—easy now," growled Pryor, stepping closer.

Willingly enough they relinquished the big cans, but as they bent to drop the powder the chance was too good to miss.

Two of them dug for their Colts. The Rio Kid, watching for that, shifted as spurts of blue-yellow came his way. The slugs narrowly missed his bobbing head in the dimness.

His own answers were joined to the reverberations of other enemy weapons. Two men screamed as the sickening thud of lead ripped their vitals. A third turned and ran, ducked low. The Rio Kid's bullet only slashed the running man's shoulder as he dived out of sight around the narrow entry to the basin, shouting at the top of his lungs.

The fourth man came to life then. He lost his head and whipped up his gun. But the Rio Kid's icy brain never faltered. He had only a minute or two in which to act, and he knew it. He shot the fourth man dead in his tracks, and sprang toward the heap of death.

Big fuses were wrapped about the containers. The Rio Kid, who had had plenty of experience with such, swiftly arranged them in succession. As he heard shouts and the poundings of many hoofs, coming toward the basin, he lit the master fuse.

Gun drawn, he waited, guarding it.

The Rio Kid was determined to destroy the terrible menace to his Lanetown friends by detonating the explosives. Pistols drawn and cocked under his thumbs, he stood in the shadow under the sliding bank, waiting for the onrushing foe. Hearing the shots and the frantic calls of their comrade, a group had quit the attack and come riding over the stream and down the east bank to the basin.

The Rio Kid had cut the master fuse short and the blue spark hissed swiftly through. It was burning briskly when several horsemen appeared in the constricted gate. Framed against the reddish sky they were fair prey for the expert marksman, the Rio Kid.

"There he is, over there!" shrieked the fellow who had run out.

Rising shotguns threatened a finale to Bob Pryor's career, but his own steady Army Colts snarled first. Two riders in the van left their saddles, the beasts they mounted rearing high and blocking off the others. Bullets whipped into the sandy slide close to the lithe Rio Kid, who stood with feet spread.

He gunned the oncoming bandits again, as they leaped the barrier, and the accuracy of his pistols smashed their nerve. The rustlers in front sought to turn, but those behind, as yet unaware who the man was they had to face, kept pushing, the half-wild mustangs biting and lashing out with their sharp hoofs.

Curses, the roar of shots rose to the sky. The Rio Kid, shooting with a deadly cold nerve, glutted the narrow entry with the dead.

His quick eye glanced at the spark. It was within seconds of the explosive point. He swung, guns snarling back, as he ran up the bank.

"There he goes!" bawled an outlaw lieutenant. "Get him!"

Surging killers pushed in, their mustangs' hoofs cutting up the wounded and dead that lay underfoot. Twenty or more were inside the constricted space as the Rio Kid flung himself, face down, on the plain above.

A tremendous explosion shook the world then. The Rio Kid was flung in a ball across the frozen ground, bruised, his brain dazed. Two more explosions, then several all together seemed to tear the universe apart.

A massive volcano of fire spewed up from what had been a rather shallow basin. Rocks and dirt, tossed high into the sky, began coming down like an infernal rain. And among them were torn and bleeding pieces of what had once been human beings.

The sound echoed and re-echoed from the hills, until it lost itself in the distance.

For an awed space following, there was stunned silence.

The Rio Kid came up on his hands and knees, crawling away by instinct. He was all in one piece, though badly bruised, and deafened.

As soon as he could, he puckered his lips and whistled several shrill bars of:

Said the Big Black Charger to the Little White Mare.

Soon Saber galloped up, nuzzled him, sniffing anxiously. Mireles had turned the horse loose, when he heard the call and, obeying orders, had retreated to hide himself.

The Rio Kid got hold of a stirrup strap and pulled himself up. He was still dazed, but got into the saddle and rode away from the creek.

He knew he had destroyed twenty, perhaps thirty of the vicious killers by use of the explosives they had intended for the innocent settlers of Lanetown.

But that hardly made an appreciable dent in the great numbers of outlaws commanded by Everts and his vicious partners.

In another way, the Rio Kid had reason to feel satisfaction. For he had worked out a grand strategy which would be communicated to Bat Masterson by Dave Garrett. And it would not be long before it would be put into execution, for already a dull, leaden streak in the eastern sky heralded the dawn.

A drink of whiskey warmed the Rio Kid, whiskey from the canteen flask he carried in his saddle-bag. The shock of the explosion was wearing off, and the pounding in his brain was lessening.

He was mounted on the fastest horse on the Frontier, never challenged successfully. With guns fresh-loaded, the Rio Kid pulled his reins and turned back toward Lanetown.

The outlaw band of attackers had drawn off from the attack on the settlement, after the ghastly explosion. Balked by the quick action of the Rio Kid from finishing the farmers off at once, Everts, Dutch Henry and Tom Owens were taking stock of the situation, passing around bottles of whiskey.

Against the gray sky, as the new dawn rapidly came up, they saw Bob Pryor, the Rio Kid. He was within rifle shot and howls of rage rose from the bandit throats.

With an impudence that further infuriated them, the Rio Kid coolly stopped Saber, threw his carbine to his shoulder, and shot a man close to Dutch Henry from his saddle. The slug had been aimed for the rustler king, but the range was long.

He moved, then, sideward, as rifles replied. Dutch Henry, maddened at sight of the lone man who was defying them, roared orders. Men leaped on their horses and the ravening pack started for the Rio Kid. He turned the dun and moved slowly away.

Bullets were plumping behind Saber's heels, kicking up bits of frozen prairie sod. Some rifle bullets whizzed uncomfortably close to the Rio Kid's bent head.

As the light grew clearer, he glanced back. The entire band was on his trail, as he had hoped. They no doubt knew by now that it was he who had been responsible for the miscarriage of their plans. They were determined to overtake him and tear him to pieces. Like a pack of furious hounds chasing a hare, they kept after him. He held Saber in enough so that they would not grow discouraged.

For ten miles as day drew on and the sun ahead showed redly, the Rio Kid led them along. When they slowed he slowed; when they spurred up, he tantalizingly kept just out of easy range. Some had dropped behind, but the main gang stayed with him.

Shouts suddenly rose from behind him, then furious answering shouts from a small band of men who rode toward him from the direction of Dodge City—Bat Masterson, with about fifteen fighters. The sheriff of Ford County, mounted on his buckskin, with guns ready, was in the lead. He called out to the Rio Kid.

The rustlers paused as they saw the reinforcements. But only fifteen men were riding to the aid of the Rio Kid, and the gunnies numbered over two hundred.

The Rio Kid galloped to Bat Masterson, who had stopped the advance of his small party. Pryor spoke to the sheriff, gesturing back at the vast crew of killers. Masterson sang out an order and the posse swung south, in swift retreat.

This settled the matter for the bandits. Shouting hoarsely, they started after the lawman's band. It was ten to one and the officers were in rout, evidently afraid to close with such a large number.

For three miles a long-range gunfight never ceased, with neither side able to make any appreciable hits. A couple of lucky shots gave slight wounds to a member or so of one faction or the other.

Ahead the plains stretched without any visible break for miles. The Arkansas was out of sight in the southern distance, with bluish low hills in the west.

The mustangs were lathered, though the air was crisp and cool. The mounts of Masterson's men seemed to be tiring fast. They had come full-tilt from Dodge City in reply to Norton Lane's alarm. So the officers rode slower, and the murderous rustlers, seeing a chance to even the score with not only the Rio Kid but with the sheriff, whom they hated, pressed avidly in for the kill.

The Rio Kid and Bat himself were at the rear of the small posse, at the post of most danger. Their guns began snarling at the eager oncoming gunnies.

"Charge!" bellowed a giant rustler chief.

Sweeping in, their blood-lust and insane fury at the Rio Kid overcoming caution the vast array of killers dug in their spurs and rode straight at the little band.

# CHAPTER XVII

## *The Battle*

☐ Moment by moment the gunfire increased in volume and fury. Bat Masterson and the Rio Kid had thrown their handful of fighting men into line, spread apart, with plenty of distance between them. The bandits were coming in red-hot, compact groups that made a ragged front some hundreds of yards in extent over the plain.

As the rustlers galloped in, expecting to overrun and quickly despatch the small party, from the earth sprang man after man, heavily armed. Each man had a rifle and two pistols, with ammunition belts over stalwart shoulders.

Point-blank, at close range, the Dodge City guns spoke.

The astounding surprise was complete. The strategy of the Rio Kid had worked out perfectly. Masterson and Pryor had led the killers into the jaws of death!

Hidden in one of the dry ravines typical of the region, ravines that were mere splits in the earth and invisible until a rider was right upon them, the main force from Dodge City had lain in waiting. At the proper moment they were ready to rise up and play the Rio Kid's game. And the guns that roared mass fire into the followers of evil were weapons that seldom missed.

116

In that line of ace fighting men Wyatt Earp's tall figure was predominant. He was shooting a light rifle, every shot making a death hit on the enemy.

Beside him coolly walked a slender, blue-eyed man with a pearl-handled Colt in his slim hand. A slight smile touched Doc Holliday's thin lips, for killing pleased him. "The most deadly gunster on the Frontier" Doc had been called, and there were few to argue the point. Uncle Billy Tilghman was present, too, doing his duty as under-sheriff of the county. His Colt barked steadily and each explosion meant a foe downed.

Neal Brown, the Cherokee breed, taciturn, fearless and unmoved, worked a Winchester as steadily as Fate itself. Bat Masterson and the Rio Kid were in the hottest of the battle.

The main force from Dodge City consisted of about one hundred and fifty. Dog Kelley had come out himself, with his shotgun. The former sergeant who had fought under Custer marched with a trained soldier's steadiness.

"Chalk" Beeson, part-owner with Dog Kelley of the Long Branch Saloon in Dodge, a big man with a walrus mustache and steady eyes, was there. The great Jim Hanrahan, buffalo hunter and plainsman extraordinary, had come out from Dodge for the shooting, for it was open season on bandits.

Billy Dixon, Wes Wilcox, Virgil Earp, Frank McLean, Charlie Bassett and others whose names made up a roster of the greatest gun-fighters on the Frontier were there. They were squad leaders in the forces raised by Bat Masterson, Dog Kelley and their allies to rally to the call of the Rio Kid.

No such array of crack marksmen, every one with nerves of cold steel, had ever before been seen.

The rustlers, coming full-tilt, ran straight into the flaming muzzles of the possemen. On foot, the men on the side of the law had steadier hands. Each picked a target—and hit it. Half the great band of outlaws took lead by the time the second volley had roared out.

The Rio Kid's grin showed his white teeth as, Colts in hand, he swept in from the flank, with Masterson and his mates, to roll up the bandit line. Riding full-tilt against the enemy, he felt at home again. This was all familiar to him, and to Saber, the dun, whose mirled eye rolled and nostrils widened at the heavy odor of burnt powder.

Terror streaked through the hearts of the killers, only a few moments before lusting for fight. They knew those men before them, were well aware of what magic they were capable with guns.

Shocked, their hands jerked viciously at the reins and the lathered mustangs skidded to halts, hoofs sliding on the frozen ground. As they checked motion, the gunfighters from Dodge took advantage of the chance to pour more bullets into them.

Dutch Henry was there, at the rear of his men. But the Rio Kid did not see Owens, and was not as yet sure of his man, Valentine Everts, whose devious trail he had so long been following.

The survivors of the rustlers swung their horses and sought retreat. But at that, the Dodge City men signaled, and aides who had been holding their mounts, somewhat rested after the run from town, in the ravine, came up with the horses. Each gun-fighter seized his animal's reins, hit leather and set out after the bandit prey.

All over the big plain individual fights occurred, as the possemen caught up with scattered groups of outlaws. Rustlers began surrendering, throwing down their guns and raising their hands. On the battlefield the wounded lay or crouched, while injured horses screamed shrilly in the cold morning air.

Masterson and the Rio Kid sped on.

"There's Dutch!" cried Bat. "I want that son!"

He threw up his Colt, emptying it after Dutch Henry who, having been well in the rear during the charge, was out front in the retreat.

"Cut down to the right, Bat!" called the Rio Kid. "I'll take the left!"

Only a few outlaws were still running and shooting. The Rio Kid saw Wyatt Earp catch up with a rustler who was bent low over his horse, get him by the scruff of the neck, and fling him off. In a fight, such men as Tilghman and Earp, Masterson, and the Rio Kid, were as good as a dozen ordinary fighters. Nothing daunted them and their minds, working swiftly, never faltering from fear or indecision, instantly told them what course to take.

Dutch Henry who had cut to the left, glanced back, his eyes glowing fearfully. The Rio Kid rested a Colt on his left arm and took careful aim. The rustler chief, the "Rob Roy of the Plains," suddenly flew from his saddle as his mount's motion checked and the horse fell dead.

Masterson yelled in triumph and swept up as the Rio Kid reached the spot. Dutch Henry lay on his face, hands outstretched, as Masterson dismounted, gun drawn.

"Reckon I'll put a finisher in the skunk," Bat growled ferociously, with a wink at the Rio Kid.

"Don't—don't shoot, Masterson!" quavered Dutch Henry. "I surrender!"

"So that's it," Masterson said.

He snapped big handcuffs on Dutch Henry. There were a couple of scratches on Dutch's face but outside of that he was only jolted and afraid. Sheriff Masterson had plenty of prisoners to take back to Dodge City but he felt a special triumph in adding Dutch Henry to the lot.

Only a remnant of beaten, fear-crazed gunmen escaped. The clever machinations of the Rio Kid, whose Army-trained brain had thought up the strategy which had given the final coup to the bandits, had been too much for them. The main gang was smashed, the survivors scattered, and riding for tall timber in the Territory and Texas.

Still the Rio Kid was not satisfied. Not as yet had he found Everts, the shadowy devil he had been after.

He had glimpsed Dave Garrett in the firing line. Garrett had followed instructions implicitly. He had ridden to meet Bat Masterson and his Dodge City posse, and given him the Rio Kid's message. The instructions had at once been understood by Masterson, for he and the Rio Kid had put the ambush ravine to skillful use on a previous occasion. It was an Indian tactic, to adopt such drywashes as cover where the timber was scarce, and Bob Pryor had suited it to his purposes.

Leaving the captives to Bat Masterson, the Rio Kid turned the dun's nose back to the ravine. He found Dave

Garrett there, nursing a slight arm wound he had taken in the swift fight.

"Hello, Dave!" the Rio Kid greeted. "Yuh shore got my message through to Bat! Where's Dupuy? Haven't lost him, have yuh?"

"No, Rio Kid. He's down in the cut, tied up like a trussed pig."

Garrett heaved his big bulk up, while the Rio Kid tied a knot in the rough bandage the young farmer had been applying to his bleeding arm. The glow of battle had died from Garrett's eyes now. They seemed steady, but dull.

The Rio Kid, followed by Garrett, slid down into the ravine, some thirty feet deep, a narrow cleft in the plain with nothing to mark it from a distance. They found Frenchy Dupuy lying there, stiff and half-frozen, hands and feet fastened, in a dither of terror.

The small man's eyes rolled up in supplication to the grim, set face of the Rio Kid whom he had come to fear above the devil himself—more than Val Everts or any man he had ever met. A coward at heart, with spying his natural profession, Frenchy Dupuy was as quivering jelly under the stern frown of the great gunfighter, the Rio Kid.

"Untie him," snarled Pryor, sticking out his lower jaw and acting for Dupuy's benefit. "I want to see him squirm, Dave."

Garrett knelt and cut the rawhides at Dupuy's wrists and ankles. Frenchy's limbs were so stiff he could scarcely move them. "No—no, don't kill me!" he begged.

"Yuh can save yore hide by talkin' and talkin' straight and fast, Dupuy," growled Pryor. "Were you in with Val Everts on that Sunrise Arms cheat back in St. Loo?"

"No—it was his, not mine," chattered Dupuy. "I—I only obeyed orders. I was his secretary there, that's all. It wasn't my fault."

"I want Everts. Where is he?"

"At Lanetown, last I saw him."

"Dutch Henry and Tom Owens work for him?"

As Dupuy gulped, the Rio Kid took a threatening step toward the cowering man.

"Yes, yes, and the whole bunch!" cried Frenchy. "They wanted to drive those farmers out of the place."

The spy had no reserve of nerve left. He spilled everything under the skillful prodding of the Rio Kid, for Bob Pryor was determined now to know the real reason why the outlaws had been so determined to exterminate the Lanetown folks.

When Frenchy had finished, the Rio Kid stood up and looked down at the little spy, scornfully. But there was no time to bother with him further now. There was work to do—for Lanetown. . . .

When the Rio Kid and his advance guard—Bat Masterson, Wyatt Earp and Doc Holliday, Dog Kelley, Neal Brown and Big Jim Hanrahan—rode to the creek ford and looked across at Lanetown, the harried citizens were out of their houses, relieved from the siege.

The remnants of the enemy had fled, including Val Everts, alias Phil Harrison, as the crooked ammunition maker had been known in Dodge.

The stocky Ben McCrory was in charge of the settlers, now that they believed Norton Lane to be dead. The powerful McCrory roared a welcome to the Rio Kid, though his usual grin was missing. He had a heavy beard stubble and dark shadows were under his blue eyes. Every man and every woman in the gathering showed the effects of the awful strain, when death had been so near them.

"So it was you who chased those devils!" bellowed McCrory, springing forward to grasp Pryor's hand. "Lane's kilt, I fear. But we ain't even found his corpse."

"He's all right," assured the Rio Kid. "He managed to get to Dodge and told us you folks had been hit. A slug cut him but he managed to grab a loose hoss and ride off. He couldn't get back to you, so he headed for Dodge."

This news cheered the settlers, but rueful glances still were cast at the burned buildings and the supplies ruined by the vandals. Stock had been shot or run off, too. Dead horses, and the bodies of several bandits still lay in the area about the remaining shacks. And they were deeply mourning the loss of some of their own men, while others were nursing wounds. They all brightened again, however, when Dave Garrett splashed his horse across the ford, and dismounted, greeting them. Everyone was happy to see the young fellow, who was a favorite with all of them.

"Which way'd they go when they left here?" demanded the Rio Kid.

Terrific as the long, running battle he had waged had proved, there burned in him a single, all-powerful determination. That was to come up with Val Everts, erstwhile president of the Sunrise Arms Company, the Phil Harrison who had been an opponent of Dog Kelley, and the instigator of the horrible surprise attack on Lanetown.

He would never rest until he caught Everts.

McCrory, in reply to the Rio Kid's query, pointed toward the low hills.

"There was only a few of 'em hangin' on the outskirts, Rio Kid. Some fellers come ridin' like sin from yore direction, and give 'em warnin'. Then they all took off into the hills, ridin' south toward the Arkansas. I reckon they're on their way to the Injun Territory."

The Rio Kid took that in soberly. The news was not to his liking. Survivors of the fight at the ravine had got away, and Everts, warned, had fled to save his own precious skin.

Expert trackers at once started on the bandit trail, but the outlaw riders had taken to the creek and had stayed in it for a time. The men from Dodge were tired, also, and their mounts had to be rested and cared for. After several miles, Masterson shook his head, pulling up his horse.

"Best thing to do," said Bat, "is rest up at Lanetown and start out tomorrer, Rio Kid. No tellin' how far we'll have to foller them skunks. And our hosses are plumb wore out."

Loath as he was to abandon the trail of Val Everts, the Rio Kid had to admit Masterson's logic. Without a full supply of ammunition and food and good horses, they would stand no chance at all of overtaking their men.

# CHAPTER XVIII

## *The Chief Devil*

☐ Hardly two hours later, with the dun refreshed and rubbed down by Celestino, and food under his own belt, after a quick nap, the Rio Kid saddled up once more.

"Where to now?" demanded Bat Masterson. "Yuh're the dangedest restlessest hombre I ever knowed, Rio Kid."

"I got a hunch, Bat. That trail was too easy at first, then it disappeared. Dupuy claims that Everts had some money cached in Dodge at his secret headquarters on the South Side. After that explosion, I figger that Everts would believe Dupuy was killed in it, and Dupuy was the only other man who savvied 'bout the cache. Everts didn't dare carry all his cash on him. He never trusted Dutch Henry and Tom Owens any too far, not with money in their sight."

"I see. Yuh think Everts will make a stab at diggin' up his kaboodle?"

"I'm shore of it. If not, I won't lose much time. They got a head start south anyways if they really kept on that way."

As he mounted, Dave Garrett came up and held out his hand.

"Good-by, Rio Kid," he said, and repeated: "The best man won. I hold no hard feelin's and want to say I've always liked you."

"Take it easy, Dave. I'll be back soon, I reckon, and we'll talk it over."

"I'm pullin' out at dawn tomorrer," Garrett said calmly. "I'm leavin' Kansas. I reckon I'll light somewheres in Texas, and start farmin' there."

The Rio Kid stared into the somber eyes. Garrett had taken what he believed to be his loss of Alice like a man. He was going away, forever. There was no saying when he would be seen again. He might change his course, drop into the wilderness, and never be heard from.

"Wait here, Dave," the Rio Kid said quickly. "Please. I'll tell her when I hit Dodge City."

Garrett shook his head. "Good-by, Rio Kid. And— good luck to you. . . ."

With eyes bloodshot from lack of sleep, and every muscle in his body aching from the terrific riding and fighting he had done, the Rio Kid drove the dun toward Dodge City. Only nerve, the steely, frigid fury of the inbred fighting man, held him up as he headed for his goal.

"I'll get him," he muttered, eyes slitted against the afternoon sun as he stared ahead over the land ocean called the prairie.

His Dodge City friends were behind him, resting up after the battle, most of them, checking prisoners, assisting the brave citizens of the tiny settlement after their long ordeal.

Dusk had fallen when he galloped over the Santa Fe tracks to the South Side, filled with its garish dives. Yellow lamps shone in the dirty windows. Saloons were opening wide for the night, and cutthroats were poking their noses out, hunting for prey.

Apprised by the cowed and terrified Dupuy of Val Everts' secrets, the Rio Kid knew just where to head. He left the dun, breathing white vapor into the cold night air, in the lee of a wooden wall for protection, and hurried down a narrow aisle to the rear of a certain dark building described to him by Frenchy Dupuy.

A sniff, and the stamp of hoofs close at hand caused him to stop. Ahead, near the rickety stoop, he could see the shape of a big black horse, saddled, waiting.

He tiptoed on. Outside the back door his eyes caught a thread of light sifting through a crack. He put an ear to the panel and heard someone moving around inside.

Suddenly the door was jerked inward and the Rio Kid found himself face to face with Val Everts, alias Phil Harrison, the man he had been after for so long.

Everts, long figure tensing, stopped short, staring into the cold-eyed fury of the man before him, his Nemesis.

Pleasure, the joy of fulfillment, thrilled through the Rio Kid's heart. For this moment he had worked long and hard. And at last he was facing the crooked contractor.

"Good evenin', Everts," he drawled. "Thought I'd find yuh here. Dupuy said there was a matter of money—and I savvied yuh never let a profit slide by."

Everts did not move as the Rio Kid stepped inside. The rangy criminal wore a six-shooter, a gold-filagreed Colt with a reversed butt, a few inches from his bony hand. The two men were not more than three feet apart.

"Well?" Everts asked quietly. "What do you want, Rio Kid?"

Pryor moved to one side a bit, turning so that he directly faced Val Everts. Bundled in heavy coats, Everts bulged at the middle. No doubt the bulge was a money belt, in which he carried stolen gains from previous crooked enterprises.

The Rio Kid was disappointed. He had expected, hoped that Val Everts would fight rather than surrender. The law was just, but such fellows could sometimes slide out of the noose.

"Yuh're my prisoner, Everts," growled Pryor.

"By what authority?"

"I'm a deputy sheriff—Bat Masterson appointed me. Besides, the Government wants yuh. I was in that Indian fight on the Niobrara when a troop of U.S. cavalry was near wiped out, thanks to dummy ammunition a skunk of a contractor sold the Army. I saw my friends suffer like heroes and die like so many flies, thanks to the Sunrise Arms Company—which was you."

Everts only glowered at him. The bony hand stayed where it was.

"Yuh son!" snarled Bob Pryor.

He went on to describe Everts in detail, but still the killer refused to go for his gun.

"I took Dupuy," the Rio Kid went on. "He spilled the beans, about Lanetown too, as well as Saint Loo. There were men killed at Lanetown and yuh'll shore stretch hemp."

Everts' upper lip curled in a sneer. There was a deep fury inside him, the reciprocal emotion to the Rio Kid's hate for the man, but he contained it. There was, as well, Everts' respect for the power and gun fighting ability of the Rio Kid.

Pryor shrugged, turned half away, putting his right hand in his pocket to draw out the makings to roll a smoke.

Everts' eyes left his arch-enemy for an instant. He saw the horse, saddled, tempting, a few feet away out the open door. He saw the occupied hands of the Rio Kid. Under his clothing he had plenty of money to maintain him in style in Mexico, where he had intended to head. An hour's start, and the tale would have been different.

It was too much for Everts to resist, the apparent bit of prime carelessness on the Rio Kid's part. Pryor's Colts hung down at his hips, while his hands were both up to light the cigarette. Everts flashed out his revolver, making a creditably swift draw.

Joy flowed through the lithe Rio Kid. Val Everts had accepted the opportunity to gain freedom!

His fingers let go of the match as his lightninglike hand was thrust inside his coat and yanked out the revolver hidden there. Everts' pistol spoke, the slug cutting at the Rio Kid's boot close to the shin.

But Pryor's Army Colt roared straight and true. Everts held for a moment, though a hole was between his murderous, burning eyes. Then his arm was falling with the weight of his weapon. He crashed, and the Rio Kid's teeth showed in his smile of victory. He had kept the vow he had sworn over young Billy Lane's body.

Pryor found Alice Lane nursing her wounded father, Norton Lane, at Dog Kelley's home. Lane was much better, was over the worst shock, and the injury was not serious. Soon he would be able to return to his friends and the new farm.

"I got some good news for yuh, Lane, at last," the Rio Kid said, smiling. "Them hills you folks have filed on are full of *galena*, which is what Val Everts was after, and why yuh was attacked by the bandits so hard. They wanted to drive yuh out and woulda kilt every man-jack of yuh if they had to, in order to take the district."

"What's *galena*?" Alice asked curiously.

"Lead—lead ore," explained the Rio Kid. "Frenchy Dupuy stumbled on it while he was hangin' around with us out there. He knows a lot about minerals—used to be an expert at it, he claims. He reported to Everts, and as Everts was sore at losin' out in Dodge and at me for helpin' to beat him, they took in Dutch Henry and his bunch and went after the hills. Dupuy says that lead's worth more than most gold mines and the hills are thick with it to the grass roots. So yuh'll be able to get rich quick and run yore farms as yuh like."

Norton Lane shook the Rio Kid's hand, his eyes beaming his gratitude.

"You've saved us, Rio Kid. Anything we have is yours. You know that."

The Rio Kid looked at Alice. She smiled at him.

"Dave Garrett's on his way to Texas," remarked Pryor. "He's startin' at dawn."

The girl's eyes instantly grew troubled. She glanced from her father to the Rio Kid.

"I wish he wouldn't go," she said, at last. "I—"

She began to cry, and quickly ran from the room. The Rio Kid trailed her, took her hand.

"Dave couldn't stand Dodge or any other town, Alice," he said gently. "He's a farmer and always will be. But that don't make him any less a fine man."

"I know it!" she choked. "I've been a fool. I—I'm sick of Dodge, too. I wish he—he hadn't gone to Texas."

"Well, he ain't started yet. And I reckon there's one thing would hold him in Kansas. That is, if yuh want to go home."

She turned her serious face up to his. He lightly touched his lips to hers.

"I do want to go home," she murmured.

"Good. Soon as I'm rested up, I'll carry the message for yuh."

He pressed her hand and strode out. . . .

The Rio Kid and Celestino Mireles overtook Dave Garrett one camp out from Lanetown. He had crossed the Arkansas but he was traveling slowly, with two led horses. The swift dun and the Mexican's new paint mount had easily come up with the young fellow.

"Hey, Dave!" sang out Pryor, as he saw his man ahea

Garrett swung in his leather, and looked surprised ɩ the Rio Kid rode up, smiling.

"Here's a note for yuh, Dave."

Garrett read the missive. The somber look in his young eyes changed, springing to hope.

"It's from Alice!" he exclaimed. "She asks me to come back—says she means to stay in Lanetown. You think she means it, Rio Kid?"

"Shore as shootin', Dave. In fact, she told me she'd rather be a farmer's wife than anything else. She's had her fling in Dodge."

Garrett began to smile, then he laughed in sheer joy. He swung his horses and started on the trail back home.

Then he remembered the Rio Kid and the Mexican and turned.

"Come on!" he called. "I got to hurry."

"We're headin' the other way, Dave."

"South?"

"Yessir." The Rio Kid stepped the dun up, shook hands with Garrett. "Good luck to yuh, boy. Mebbe we'll meet again. The Frontier's big, but when we ride this way, I'll look yuh up."

"So long, Rio Kid—and thanks a million."

The Rio Kid's white teeth gleamed in a smile. He watched Garrett dig in his spurs and gallop back—to Alice.

Then he swung the dun and cantered, with Mireles at his flank, toward the wilds. Restless and footloose, fancy free, the Rio Kid ranged the Frontier.